A CHILDREN'S TREASURY of MYTHOLOGY

A CHILDREN'S TREASURY of MYTHOLOGY

ILLUSTRATED BY
MARGARET EVANS PRICE

BARNES & NOBLE
NEW YORK

Originally published as *A Child's Book of Myths and Enchantment Tales*

2007 Barnes & Noble, Inc.

Barnes & Noble, Inc.
122 Fifth Avenue
New York, NY 10011

ISBN-13: 978-0-7607-9428-9

Printed and bound in China

3 5 7 9 10 8 6 4 2

CONTENTS

FOREWORD

Over 2,000 years ago, Greek and Roman grandmothers and grandfathers told magnificent stories to their grandchildren. These stories were already old, having been handed down from time before memory. Yet their grace and freshness make them as magnificent today as they were then.

Many of these stories are myths about nature, imagined out of the wonder people felt for things they could not explain. Apollo drives the sun chariot across the sky every day, except when he goes hunting and leaves the sun hidden behind the clouds. Atlas' hips form the slopes of a mighty mountain; his hair and beard become forests and the weight of the sky rests on his shoulders after regarding Medusa's head. Proserpina is captured by Pluto, thus explaining the turning of the seasons.

Children who today know the scientific reasons for the sun's and moon's seeming movement across our sky, who know why the seasons change and what the stars are, still can feel the wonder felt by ancient storytellers. For the world is still wondrous, no matter how clear our knowledge.

Some stories are myths touching on history and geography—Prometheus giving fire to mortals; Helle falling from the golden-fleeced ram's back at a place thereafter called Hellespont; Bellerophon's travels while riding on the winged back of Pegasus.

Magic and enchantment abound in these stories. Medea's magic helps Jason tame wild animals as surely as Circe's enchantment changes Ulysses' friends into animals. Minerva, the gray-eyed goddess, watches over heroes and gives wisdom and skill to all those who truly wish it. Gods and goddesses give magic to mortals to help them out of all kinds of difficulties, and sometimes to put them into difficulties.

With the magic, there is truth. Brave, strong heroes such as Jason and Hercules, like today's readers, sometimes feel despair. Atalanta, a fleet-footed heroine, would be worthy of a modern Olympic medal. Cupid's arrows touch people to love, sometimes making them seem silly, but often giving them profound concern for one another, and Cupid manages to inflict even himself with love. Gods' and people's faults are shown as well as their virtues. Phaeton's overreaching pride and Pandora's obsessive curiosity cause disasters; but Pygmalion and Galatea, humble in their thanks to Venus, live happily ever after.

For many good reasons, then, these classic tales live on. Most are Greek tales. A couple, namely "Pomona and Vertumnus" and "Pygmalion and Galatea" are of Roman origin. In this edition, these stories are reprinted from *A CHILD'S BOOK OF MYTHS*, 1924, and *ENCHANTMENT TALES FOR CHILDREN*, 1926, both graced with the gentle art of Margaret Evans Price. These versions of the ageless myths and enchantment tales are as clear and beautiful today as they were in the 1920s.

In the first edition, in 1924, Katherine Lee Bates wrote words still appropriate: "Do not say these stories are too beautiful to be true. They are too beautiful *not* to be true.... Let them persuade you that you and all about you, home and school and out-of-doors, the lives you live and the world in which you live them, are made up of beauty and marvel and splendor.... The only thing that does not exist is the commonplace."

THE EDITORS

PLUTO SEIZED PROSERPINA BY THE WRIST

PROSERPINA AND PLUTO

Pluto was god of Erebus, the world that lies beneath the ground. In his realm all was dark, misty, and gloomy. There was no sunshine there, nor any light except the glow of fires. Instead of blue sky overhead, he had only a roof of damp and dripping earth. There were no gay-colored flowers in his kingdom, nor tall branching trees, nor green grass.

In some places the dripping water mingled with rust-colored lime from the earth, and hardened into all sorts of shapes. It made columns and arches and mounds, or hung like icicles in long, thin pendants from the roofs of Pluto's many caverns. There were black marble rocks in Erebus, and deep, dark lakes.

It would have been a dreary place for an earth child, but Pluto thought his kingdom the most beautiful in the world.

He thought his caves hung with lime crystals far lovelier than forests of birch trees. He liked the noiseless peace of the dim caverns. No songs of birds, no rustle of wind among the trees, disturbed their quiet. Only at times he heard far off the barking of Cerberus, who guarded the entrance to his kingdom.

To drive away the dampness in the caves, Pluto lit many fires. Their flickering flames made the lime crystals sparkle and glimmer on the dark waters of the lakes. These fires were silent, too. They never crackled cheerfully as earth fires do.

The god of this strange, quiet land was content to stay in his own kingdom and seldom journeyed to the earth, which seemed a noisy place after the deep silence of Erebus.

PLUTO, THE GOD OF THIS STRANGE QUIET LAND, WAS
CONTENT TO STAY IN HIS OWN KINGDOM

But once Jupiter imprisoned four great giants in a cavern in Mount Aetna. In their anger the giants stamped their feet and shook the earth, raging back and forth and beating on the walls of their prison, or heaving their mighty shoulders against the sides of the cavern until the mountain trembled.

Far off in his kingdom under the ground Pluto heard these strange rumblings and feared that from the shock the surface of the earth might crack and the light of day break through.

So, mounting his chariot drawn by four black horses, he journeyed swiftly up to earth and rode here and there to see how much damage had been done by the angry giants.

He found temples overturned, trees uprooted, and rocks thrown about as though some great earthquake had shaken the land, but no cracks deep enough to disturb the gloom of Erebus.

Pluto was preparing to return home, for the light of the sun was painful to his eyes, and he did not like the strange perfume of the earth flowers nor the sound of wind in the trees. But Cupid, that mischievous god of love, had other plans for Pluto.

He drew his bow, wounding the god of darkness with one of those arrows which cause the wounded one to love the first person he meets.

Pluto had just grasped the reins of his four black horses to turn them homeward, when he saw Proserpina, the daughter of Ceres, with half a dozen nymphs, dancing across the valley. Proserpina's hair floated behind her, bright as a flame of golden fire, and her eyes were as black as Pluto's lakes. She came nearer, gathering flowers and twining them into garlands.

The god of the dark kingdom stepped from his chariot and left it hidden among the trees. His cloak waved about him in many points and folds, thin and fluttering like a garment of smoke. Little tongues of fire rose from his crown and flickered above his forehead.

Proserpina and the nymphs saw him and drew back in alarm. Pluto strode toward them and seized Proserpina by the wrist. He did not woo her gently and kindly as lovers do. He said nothing at all, but lifted her in his arms and carried her off into the forest. Stepping into his chariot, he seized the reins with one hand, and held Proserpina with the other. The four black horses sprang forward with a bound, galloping madly away toward the river Cyane.

Proserpina screamed for help. She cried to Ceres, her mother, but Pluto urged on his horses, and the chariot dashed away still faster.

When they reached the edge of the river Cyane, Pluto commanded the waters to open so that he might pass, but the river nymph saw that Proserpina was being carried away, and refused to help Pluto or make a pathway for him to cross.

Then in anger Pluto struck the ground with his mighty three-pronged spear, and the earth itself opened. The horses plunged downward, and with the chariot rattling from side to side, disappeared in the darkness.

Now, far off, Ceres had heard Proserpina's cry as Pluto carried her away. A sharp pain shot through the mother's heart, and like a bird she flew through forest and valley, seeking Proserpina. She climbed mountains and crossed rivers, asking everyone she met for tidings of Proserpina, but neither man nor god would tell her where Pluto had carried her daughter.

A long, dark cloak hid Ceres' face and the brightness of her hair. No one who saw her then would have known that she was the glowing goddess of the harvest. For many days she wandered over the earth, refusing in her sorrow to taste either ambrosia or nectar.

A LONG DARK CLOAK HID THE BRIGHTNESS OF CERES' HAIR

Once, as she sat on a stone resting beside a well, the four daughters of Celeus, running and leaping like young gazelles, came to fill their pitchers.

They saw the aged woman at the spring. Her head was bent in sorrow, and her dark mantle spoke of mourning. They touched her gently on the shoulder and asked her why she grieved, but Ceres did not tell them or let them know that she was a goddess. She let them think she was only an aged woman in trouble.

THE FOUR DAUGHTERS OF CELEUS, RUNNING AND LEAPING LIKE YOUNG GAZELLES,
CAME TO FILL THEIR PITCHERS AT THE WELL

When their pitchers were filled, they put their arms around Ceres and led her home. Everyone in the house of Celeus was so gentle and kind that Ceres found comfort in her sorrow.

Celeus had an infant son who fell ill while Ceres rested in his home. The goddess nursed the little boy and gave him heavenly gifts, so that he grew in strength and beauty and wisdom.

Celeus and his family begged the visitor to live with them always, but Ceres wandered on, still seeking for Proserpina.

At last she came to the banks of the river Cyane, but the river nymph, fearing the anger of Pluto, dared not tell Ceres where the missing Proserpina was hidden.

Now it happened that as Pluto's horses had dashed down into the earth, Proserpina's girdle, loosened by her struggle to free herself, fell from the chariot and lay on the river bank.

THE NYMPHS SHIVERED AND WRAPPED THEIR ROBES
AROUND THEM

The river nymph now took this girdle and floated it to where Ceres stood mourning at the water's edge.

Ceres saw it, and now her grief was more terrible than ever. She took away her blessing from the earth and cast an evil spell on the fruits and crops.

The leaves of the trees lost their green and began to fall in clouds of yellow. The blue sky grew angry and gray, and a cold wind swept over the earth. The nymphs shivered and wrapped their thin robes around them.

Everything became dry and withered, and famine and sickness and grief were over the whole earth.

Then the fountain, Arethusa, spoke to Ceres and told her where Proserpina was. "I come from far down in the earth," sang the fountain. "My waters have trickled through the realms of Pluto. I have seen your daughter. I have seen Proserpina, the beautiful, the bright, sitting on a black marble throne, queen of the spirits which wander silently between the crystal pillars and the flickering fires, and float over the lakes from which my waters rise."

When Ceres heard this, she raised her arms to Jupiter and begged him to return Proserpina to the earth.

"Never again," she cried, "will I make the corn grow or the ripening grain bend in golden waves. Unless my daughter is restored to me, never again will I watch over the harvest. The fruits of the earth shall remain withered, and man die from hunger."

Jupiter feared that Ceres would do as she threatened, so he sent Mercury, the speedy messenger, to fly swiftly to Pluto, and bid him release Proserpina.

"But if she has eaten in Erebus even I cannot take her from Pluto," said Jupiter.

When Mercury went down into the kingdom of darkness, he took

MERCURY, THE SPEEDY MESSENGER OF THE GODS

Spring with him. They flew over the river Styx and passed Cerberus, the three-headed dog. When Cerberus, his three great jaws wide open, sprang at them, Spring loosed her mantle and shook such a shower of white petals in his face that he could not see. His mouths were filled with them, and they clung to the lashes of his eyes. Some fell into the river Styx and floated on the dark water.

"They are like the fair queen, Proserpina, on her black marble throne," said Charon, the boatman.

"Such a dreary place to keep the daughter of Ceres!" thought Mercury, as they flew through the gloomy caverns and passages toward Pluto's palace.

Soon Pluto began to notice a faint fragrance which reminded him of the earth world above. He frowned, and hurried to the doors of his palace. Proserpina felt the mild warmth and followed.

They saw Mercury approaching, with Spring floating at his side. "Rejoice, O daughter of Ceres," said Mercury, "for Jupiter bids you return to earth, which lies brown and barren because of grief over your loss."

Pluto frowned more fiercely than ever. "She has eaten six seeds of a pomegranate," he said. "The fates decree that whoever eats in Erebus never may leave."

"But only six little seeds!" begged Proserpina. "There are twice six months in the year. Only let me see my mother! Let me feel the warm sunshine and soft winds, and gather flowers again, and I will come back to you!"

Pluto had grown to love Proserpina dearly. He could not bear to lose her forever, yet he wished her to be happy. So he agreed to let her go back to her mother for six months of the year, but the other six she promised to spend with him.

With Spring on one side and Mercury on the other, Proserpina journeyed up to earth, where Ceres awaited her.

As the ground opened to let them out, the cold winds hurried away beyond the sea. Ceres dropped her mantle of gray and laughed with

"PROSERPINA HAS EATEN SIX SEEDS OF A POMEGRANATE"

joy to hold her daughter once more in her arms. The bare branches burst into bud, and tiny leaves sprang from every twig. Starry white flowers sprinkled the moss, and the perfume of Spring filled the forest.

Mercury flew back to Mount Olympus, but Spring began her journey over the earth to star the fields with blossoms and carry the tidings that Proserpina had come back.

ATALANTA AND HIPPOMENES

~ 20 ~

Atalanta was a Greek maiden who could run faster than any one on earth. She could outrun the winds, Boreas and Zephyr. Only Mercury, with his winged sandals, ran more swiftly.

Besides being so fleet-footed, Atalanta was very beautiful, and many Greek youths from every part of the kingdom wished to marry her. But Atalanta did not wish to marry any one and turned them all away, saying, "I shall be the bride only of him who shall outrun me in the race, but death must be the penalty of all who try and fail."

In spite of this hard condition there still were a few brave suitors willing to risk their lives for a chance of winning Atalanta.

For one of the races the runners chose the youth Hippomenes for judge.

Hippomenes felt both pity and scorn for the runners. He thought they were foolish to risk their lives, and bade them go home. He reminded them that the land was full of lovely maidens who were kinder and more gentle than Atalanta.

"But you have not yet seen Atalanta," said one of the suitors to Hippomenes. "You do not know all her beauty and loveliness. See, she comes!"

HIPPOMENES

Hippomenes looked, and saw Atalanta as she drew near. She laid aside her cloak and made ready for the race. For a moment she stood poised like a graceful white bird about to fly.

The suitors who stood beside her trembled with fear and eagerness.

At a word from Hippomenes the runners were off, but at the first step Atalanta flew ahead. Her tunic fluttered behind her like a banner. Her hair, loosened from its ribbon, blew about her shoulders in bright waves.

As she ran, Hippomenes thought her very beautiful and became envious of the runner who might win her. He shouted praises when she reached the goal far ahead of her poor suitors.

Hippomenes forgot that the penalty of failure was death. He did not remember the advice he had given the other runners to go home and forget the loveliness of Atalanta. He knew only that he loved her and must himself race with her.

Raising his head toward Mount Olympus, he prayed to Venus, the goddess of love, and asked her to help him.

As he stood beside Atalanta, waiting the signal for the race to start, Venus appeared to him and slipped three golden apples into his hands.

"Throw them one by one in Atalanta's path," whispered Venus.

The goddess was invisible to everyone but Hippomenes. No one saw her as she gave him the apples, nor heard her as she told him what to do with them.

Atalanta looked pityingly at the handsome youth as he stood ready to run. She was sorry for him, and for a moment she hesitated and almost wished that he might win the race.

The signal was given, and Atalanta and Hippomenes flew swiftly over the sand. Atalanta was soon ahead, but Hippomenes, sending up a prayer to Venus, tossed one of his golden apples so that it fell directly in front of Atalanta.

Astonished at the beautiful apple which seemed to fall from nowhere, she stooped to pick it up.

That instant Hippomenes passed her, but Atalanta, holding the apple firmly in her hand, at once darted ahead. Again she outdistanced Hippomenes. Then he threw the second apple.

Atalanta could not pass without picking it up, and then, because of the apple in her other hand, paused a moment longer. When she looked up, Hippomenes was far ahead.

But gaining, she overtook and passed him. Then, just before she reached the goal, he threw the third apple.

ATALANTA STOOPED TO PICK UP THE GOLDEN APPLE

"I can win easily," thought Atalanta, "even though I stoop for this other apple." As she was already holding an apple in each hand, she paused just for an instant as she wondered how to grasp the third.

That moment Hippomenes shot past, reaching the goal before Atalanta.

Amid the wild shouts of those who watched, he wrapped the maiden's cloak around her shoulders and led her away. Hippomenes was so happy that he forgot to thank the goddess Venus, who followed them to the marriage feast.

Invisible, she moved among the wedding guests. She saw Atalanta place the golden apples in a bowl of ivory and admire their beauty, but Hippomenes, in his delight, thought no more of the apples or of the goddess who had given them to him.

Venus was angry with Hippomenes for being so thoughtless, and instead of blessing the lovers she caused them to be changed into a lion and a lioness, doomed forever to draw the chariot of Cybele, the mother of Jupiter, through the heavens and over the earth.

ADMETUS AND ALCESTIS

Once, on an April morning when the skies of Greece were their bluest and the violets beside the river Amphrysus only a shade duller than the sky, when the young white lambs were wild with gayety and happiness, King Admetus rode forth to see his flocks.

The king's herdsmen and shepherds bowed before him as he rode through the green pastures and down the beautiful valleys.

Most kingly he looked, with the glory of the spring sun on his fair hair, and his many-hued mantle fluttering behind like a banner in the wind.

Now and then he reined his great horse and spoke with a shepherd or watched the lambs and ewes.

At length, following the river as he rode, he beheld a strange shepherd sitting alone by the stream, playing on a lyre and singing to himself. As he bent his golden head above his lyre, the sheep which he should have watched were straying to the farthest ends of the field.

He was so intent upon his song that he did not hear the steps of the king's horse, thudding softly on the moist grass, but continued to sing and touch the strings of his lyre, while King Admetus sat silent and listened.

The shepherd's music was so lovely that tears came to the king's eyes, and he felt as though his heart would break. The young king's thoughts turned to his beloved Alcestis, the daughter of King Pelias.

ADMETUS BEHELD A STRANGE SHEPHERD SITTING ALONE BY THE STREAM, PLAYING ON A
LYRE AND SINGING TO HIMSELF

Admetus and Alcestis had loved each other since their first meeting. No other suitor seemed to Alcestis so noble or so kingly, and she would gladly have gone with him to his palace to be his bride and rule with him over Thessaly, but Pelias, her father, loved her so mightily and so selfishly that he could not bear to have her leave him even to marry the beloved of her heart.

King Pelias planned a way to keep all suitors from winning Alcestis. He promised her to the lover who would come to claim her riding in a chariot drawn by lions and boars.

No mortal suitor could tame or harness these fierce beasts, so Pelias thought that he was sure to keep his lovely daughter forever with him.

But even his cleverest plans could not lessen the love of Alcestis for Admetus, nor prevent her from thinking of him and longing for him.

As for King Admetus, every beautiful sight, every lovely sound,

THE STRANGER WAS BEAUTIFUL BEYOND THE
BEAUTY OF MORTAL SHEPHERD

recalled Alcestis to his mind, and never had he felt so close to her as when he heard the strange shepherd playing by the river. It was as if Alcestis rode at his side. He could see her glorious smile, warm as the spring sun, and her lovely eyes, blue as the violets around his horse's feet.

As Zephyr, the soft wind, with a gentle rustle passed through the trees, the waving and bending of the tall grass marking his pathway, Admetus could almost feel the silken touch of Alcestis' hair blown across his cheek, there was such magic in the shepherd's playing.

"Arise, strange shepherd!" cried the king. "Who art thou, and from what land comest thou to tend my flocks?"

The shepherd looked up and, seeing the king, arose. He was taller than Admetus, broader of shoulder, and beautiful beyond the beauty of mortal shepherd.

"He is more like a prince than a herder of flocks," thought Admetus.

"Who art thou?" he asked again.

The stranger bowed his head and answered humbly, "Thy servant, King Admetus."

Now the king was wise and skilled in reading the hearts of men, and he guessed that this was no servant but perhaps some noble youth or even a god.

He bade the shepherd follow him, and set another, more lowly but more watchful, to herd the straying flocks.

He led the stranger to his palace and gave him a white linen robe, taking away his ragged tunic. His maidens set food before the shepherd, serving him with bread and honey and the juice of grapes.

When he had finished eating, Admetus bade him play again. Once more the youthful shepherd touched his lyre, and again the king felt the near presence of his beloved like a perfume beside him.

Day after day the shepherd dwelt with the king, singing or playing his lyre at his master's command. They walked together over the flower-strewn fields or rode beside the river, king and shepherd, talking and singing and watching the lambs.

Admetus gave the stranger the stewardship over all the other shepherds and over all his flocks, and indeed, although he seemed at first a careless shepherd to let his sheep stray and wander where they chose, yet he had a strange power over all the flocks. An ailing ewe became well at the touch of his hands. The lambs in King Admetus' flocks grew as no other lambs ever before had grown. Their fleece was white and soft like creamy silk, and not one lamb perished or strayed too far beyond the safety of the valley.

The king grew exceedingly fond of the shepherd and, walking with him in the fields, told him his most beautiful thoughts. He spoke of his love for Alcestis and of the hopelessness of winning her.

"How can any mortal harness lions and boars, or train them to draw a chariot?" he asked.

The shepherd smiled, and agreed that it was not a task for mortals.

The next day the chief shepherd was missing. Admetus thought sadly that his last blessing, his greatest human comfort, had vanished from him. He thought the gracious singer had gone on to other realms. The king then gave himself up to sorrow, and walked no more among his flocks nor rode beside the river Amphyrus, where first he had found the noble shepherd.

ADMETUS LEAPED INTO THE CHARIOT AND DROVE OFF IN A CLOUD OF WHITE DUST

Instead, he sat in his courtyard grieving now for both Alcestis and his friend. The roses in his garden flung their perfume toward him. The birds sang, the tall, dark cedars cast their lovely blue and purple shadows on the ivory pillars of his palace and gave back their images in the garden pool, but Admetus did not lift his head or cease grieving.

At last one day came a shouting and wild commotion. Servants burst through his high garden gates, screaming in terror.

"Lions are coming, and boars!" they cried. "Run! Run!"

They were so frightened that they did not look twice, or they would have seen the chariot, the harness, and the driver who held the reins of those strange beasts that came running toward the palace.

King Admetus rose and went to shut the gates of the garden. Looking down the broad white road, he saw the shepherd whom he loved, driving his chariot toward the palace. He saw the lions and boars harnessed together, and knew that now he might go to ask for Alcestis.

His heart leaped to meet the shepherd, and his feet carried him toward the chariot with the speed of the wind.

Forgetting that he was king, the other a servant, he embraced his beloved shepherd and thanked him, then leaped into the chariot and drove off in a cloud of white dust toward the kingdom of Pelias.

He made no stops on the long journey, though his throat was dry with the dust of the road, and the vineyards wh ich he passed hung heavy with cooling grapes; though the wayside fountains splashed crystal and clear, and the shade of the tall trees invited him to refreshing rest.

Only when he neared the kingdom of Pelias did he pause. Then, still holding the reins of his strange steeds, he bent over a little stream and washed the dust from his brow, the stains from his hands, that Alcestis might see him, not as a dusty traveler, but as a king.

Now it happened that Alcestis on that day sat weaving in her tower with her maidens about her. She moved her shuttle back and forth, blending bright-hued threads into lovely patterns, thinking of her lover, and hoping, as maidens do, that her handiwork, the web in the loom, might find a place in his palace if ever the gods were kind and she went to be the bride of King Admetus. As she worked, a maiden idling near the window cried out and pointed down the road.

There, speeding toward the palace, Alcestis beheld Admetus in his chariot drawn by those fierce beasts which her father thought never might be driven together, now tamed and broken to harness and bringing her beloved swiftly nearer and nearer to her side.

She dropped her shuttle. The colored yarns fell from her lap in a bright heap to the floor. Calling her father, down from her tower she ran, and out into the courtyard, to meet Admetus.

Great was King Pelias' sorrow that Alcestis must leave him, but he kept his word, and that evening Admetus and Alcestis were wed.

In the morning Admetus led his bride to the strange chariot. He touched one of the great lions on the head, and the beast fawned and drooped his neck as a gentle horse might do. He spoke to the boars, and they rubbed their heads against him.

He lifted Alcestis into the chariot and drove away to his own kingdom, where the shepherd awaited them.

The palace was wreathed and garlanded with flowers. A banquet lay ready, and sweet music strayed through the hallways and chambers. The shepherd had prepared everything for the homecoming of Alcestis. Thereafter the king loved the shepherd more dearly than ever.

Peace and perfect happiness reigned in the palace of Admetus. It was as if the blessing of some god had fallen on King Admetus, so that everything he touched seemed to prosper. His flocks increased wonderfully. His harvests were rich beyond belief, and love and joy filled his heart.

But one day Admetus fell ill. Not one of the wise men in his kingdom could cure him or tell his ailment. The shepherd laid aside his lyre and stayed by the king's couch. He comforted Alcestis and helped her as she nursed Admetus.

But here that skill which had cured the sick ewes seemed powerless. The king grew worse, and sorrow fell upon the palace.

One evening the shepherd arose and went away, saying nothing of his purpose. Then, indeed, if any had watched him as he departed, they would have known that the strange shepherd was more than mortal.

CLOTHO, LACHESIS, AND ATROPOS

Rising into the air, he disappeared in the low-hanging sunset clouds. He flew with great speed to the cavern of the Three Fates, Clotho, Lachesis, and Atropos.

It was Clotho who spun the bright threads of youth, Lachesis who wound them on her spindle, and Atropos, the eldest, who cut them with her slender shears.

As the shepherd entered their cave, the aged Atropos raised her head and blinked, as one who is blinded by the sunlight, but the younger Fates smiled and turned joyfully toward the visitor.

"Apollo, god of the sun, why do you come to our cavern?" croaked Atropos.

"O Atropos," said Apollo, he who seemed but a shepherd on earth, "O Atropos, you hold in your hands a life thread which you are about to cut. Stay your hand and return your thread to Lachesis, that King Admetus may live!"

Clotho and Lachesis, seeming to agree with their glorious visitor, held out their hands to stay their sister as she held her shears ready to close upon the slender life thread of King Admetus.

"I will spare him," croaked Atropos, "if some one else will die in his stead."

"There are many who would do that," answered Apollo.

"Find one before nightfall," warned Atropos as Apollo flew away.

He hurried to the palace and told the courtiers and servants that the king might live if one of them would die.

"Die for him yourself, young shepherd," said one. But Apollo, being an immortal, could not do this. He went all over the palace, except to the chamber where Admetus lay, looking for some one who loved Admetus enough to die for him. He sought in the farthest borders of the kingdom. Everyone was sorry to hear that the king was dying, but he found no one who was willing to give up his own life to save him.

The afternoon was almost gone, and Apollo, grieving and heart-sick, went to the chamber of the king.

Alcestis sat beside him, tired and very white. Apollo told her what he had told everyone in the kingdom.

"Let me die for him!" said Alcestis. "Oh, I am so glad that he will live!"

Immediately, far away in their lonely home, the Three Fates heard. At the same moment Admetus opened his eyes and smiled at Alcestis.

A little glow of pink came into his cheeks, and strength returned to him, but every hour Alcestis grew whiter, until soon she lay on the couch from which Admetus had risen.

When the king heard that she had offered to die in his place, he wished that he might be ill again, and Alcestis well, but the promise had been given, and nothing could be done.

Now it happened just at this time that Hercules, the strongest of heroes, was passing through the country and stopped at the palace to rest. He heard the sounds of mourning, and was told that the lovely queen Alcestis was dying. He asked the servants to show him her chamber, and with a grim look on his face he sat down outside her door. For hours he sat there waiting. The people of the palace walked past him on tiptoe and wondered why he watched at the door.

"LET ME DIE FOR HIM!" SAID ALCESTIS. "OH, I AM SO GLAD THAT HE WILL LIVE!"

No sound came from the room. Everything was quiet.

At last the sky grew dark, and Death, the messenger of Atropos, entered the palace to carry away the spirit of Alcestis. Through the wide gates he passed, invisible, and up the marble stairs. Like a rude winter wind he swept down the corridor to Alcestis' door.

Hercules felt him coming and arose to meet him. He stretched his arms across the door, and as Death tried to press past him, he caught him and wrestled with him.

At the touch of Hercules, Death became visible. His black garments whirled about them in great folds as they fought. When a bit of cloth so much as touched Hercules, he felt as if an icy branch had struck him. When he seized Death by the throat, it was like grasping a huge icicle.

At last Hercules overcame Death and threw him rattling out of the palace, his black garments torn to shreds and half his bones broken.

He limped back to Atropos, and no amount of commanding or threatening would induce him to return.

The color came flooding back into the white cheeks of Alcestis. She sat up, and, feeling strength stealing back to her limbs, arose from her couch and smiled upon King Admetus. The king was wild with happiness. Again and again he poured out his thanks to Hercules and to his beloved shepherd.

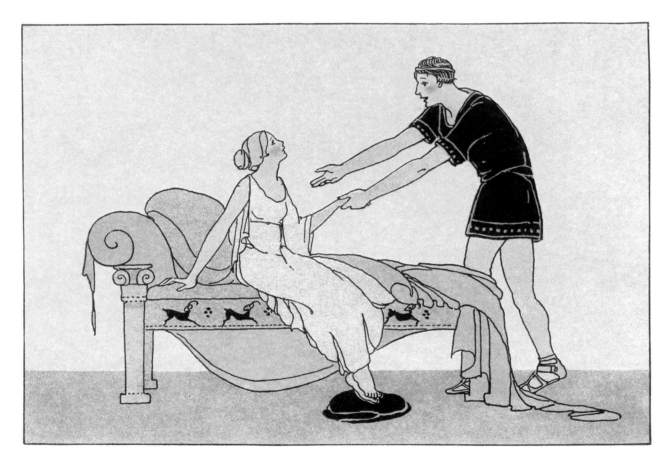

ALCESTIS SAT UP AND SMILED UPON KING ADMETUS

Thereafter, when Hercules passed through the kingdom, it was as if all things therein belonged to him, and as if the palace were his own, so great were the honors that Admetus showered upon him.

As for the mysterious shepherd, so tall and strangely noble, so full of power and gifts, Hercules looked on him and knew him for Apollo. He bowed before him in the presence of the king, and Apollo, knowing that he could conceal himself no longer, laid aside the earthly garments which he wore, and shone before them, glorious, blinding, and beautiful beyond the beauty of mortals.

And now he must return to Olympus. His year upon the earth was over. He had brought happiness and love and life itself to Admetus and Alcestis, so, bidding them farewell with many blessings, he left them and flew back to Olympus to his heavenly tasks.

HERCULES

When Hercules was a baby he lived in the palace of
Amphitryon, king of Thebes. Although Amphitryon
loved the baby dearly and provided many women to wait
on him and care for him, Hercules was not his own child. He was the son
of the great god Jupiter, king of the heavens.

BABY HERCULES AND THE SERPENT

King Amphitryon was proud of him because he was much larger
and stronger than other babies, but Juno, who was the wife of Jupiter and
queen of all the goddesses, hated this little son of Jupiter.

One day the goddess sent two great serpents to destroy Hercules as
he lay in his cradle, but Hercules wakened as the serpents rustled over

HERCULES RETURNED CARRYING THE BODY OF THE GREAT BEAST

his linen coverlet, and, reaching out his strong little hands, he grasped them round the neck and held them tight until they were strangled. His nurses, hearing him crow, knew his nap was over, so they came in to take him up. There lay the two serpents dead in his cradle!

This was such a wonderful thing for a baby to do, that King Amphitryon boasted of it all over his kingdom. As Hercules grew older, the king searched far and wide until he found the wisest teachers to train him in all the ways in which a prince should be trained.

In one way his nurses and teachers had a hard time with Hercules. He had so terrible a temper that when he became angry everyone ran out of his reach. King Amphitryon tried in many ways to teach Hercules to control his temper, but it was no use. One day his music teacher, whose name was Linus, reproved him for carelessness and tried to punish him. Hercules at once raised his lute and struck Linus on the head. The blow was such a terrible one that Linus died.

After that Hercules was in disgrace with King Amphitryon, and the king sent him away to live among his herdsmen and the cattle.

In the mountains where the king's herds were kept, there lived a lion which kept carrying off the fattest cows. Often, too, it had killed a herdsman. Soon after Hercules came to live in the mountains, he killed this lion, and in other ways made himself so useful to the herdsmen that they grew to love him, and held him in great respect.

Hercules continued to grow larger and stronger, and at last he returned to Thebes and fought for the king against his enemies. He won many victories for King Amphitryon, who forgave him for killing Linus.

The rest of his life Hercules spent in twelve adventures that were full of danger. Among them was his fight with a terrible lion which lived in the valley of Nemea. When he failed to kill it with his club, he strangled it with his hands, and returned carrying the body of the great beast across his shoulders.

Next he killed a nine-headed water serpent called the Hydra, which lived in the country of Argos, and then he captured a boar that had long overrun the mountains of Arcadia, frightening and killing the people.

From one of his adventures he returned bringing a wonderful stag, with antlers of gold and feet of brass, which dwelt in the hills about Arcadia.

Whenever Hercules heard of a monster that preyed on the people, he at once set out to overcome it. Sometimes he was sent on these dangerous adventures by Juno, who still wished that harm might befall him, but Hercules had the help of Jupiter and each time returned victorious.

He was sent to clean the stables of King Augeas, who had a herd of three thousand oxen, whose stalls had not been cleaned in thirty years.

Hercules cleverly thought of a way to clean the filthy stables without even entering them. He dug a wide ditch from a river to the stables, and let the waters rush through the stalls into a ditch on the other side and down the hill into another river.

In a few hours the stables were clean. Then Hercules walled up the opening between the first river and the ditch so that no more water could flow through. When King Augeas came to look at his stables, much to his astonishment he found them clean and dry.

Hercules was also sent to find the golden apples which were guarded by the three daughters of Hesperus and by a great dragon which coiled itself among the trees of the garden.

Hercules knew that Atlas owned the gardens of the Hesperides, so he journeyed to the mountain of Atlas and asked him if he would not like to rest from the weight of the sky, which he had held on his great shoulders ever since Perseus turned him into stone.

Hercules offered, with Jupiter's help, to change Atlas back into a

THE THREE DAUGHTERS OF HESPERUS GUARDING THE GOLDEN APPLES

giant, so that he might walk the earth and wade in cool streams and rest in green valleys. This he would do if Atlas would agree to go to his garden and gather some golden apples for him. Atlas was eager to be released from the burden of the sky and the stars, and promised to do anything Hercules wished if only he might once more be free.

So Hercules took the weight of the heavens on his own shoulders and Atlas stepped out, shaking his head wildly, shouting and leaping with gladness at being free once more. He went joyously across the land, splashing through cool streams and striding through the green grass.

Hercules held the heavens until Atlas finally returned with his big hands and deep pockets filled with golden apples. Atlas begged that he

HERCULES HELD UP THE HEAVENS

might carry them to Hercules' land and deliver them. But Hercules was afraid that if Atlas went he might never come back, so he asked Atlas to hold the earth until he rested his shoulders. He then set the sky again on the giant's shoulders and went back to Thebes with the golden apples.

In spite of his temper Hercules was kind, and learning that Prometheus was still chained to the rock where Jupiter had bound him, he urged his father to give him permission to break the chains which held Prometheus, and set him free. Jupiter agreed, and Prometheus, after his long punishment, was unbound.

At last, after many glorious labors, Hercules was carried to Mount Olympus in Jupiter's own chariot, and became one of the Immortals.

CUPID AND APOLLO

~

Cupid was the baby son of Venus. Although his mother fed him daily with nectar and ambrosia, the food of the gods, he never seemed to grow. The years passed by, and still Cupid remained a tiny, dimpled, laughing child, although he could fly and run wherever he wished and care for himself on earth as well as on Mount Olympus.

When Apollo was not driving his chariot, Cupid loved to follow him around, for he was more fond of Apollo than of any of the other gods. He was much interested in Apollo's bow and arrows and longed to take them in his hand.

Once he saw Apollo take his strongest bow and his sharpest arrows and set out to kill a huge, dark monster called the Python.

The Python was a gloomy creature that breathed heavy black smoke from his nostrils. This filled the air for miles around with darkness, and the shadows were so heavy that no one standing in the valley could see the mountain tops.

As Apollo was the god of light, he did not like the darkness, so he went straight into the shadowy valley, found the terrible Python, and killed him.

Cupid followed him so quietly that Apollo did not know he was there until after the Python was killed, and the darkness had lifted from the valley. Then he saw the boy standing beside him.

"Oh, your arrows are wonderful!" cried Cupid. "Give me one! I'll do anything you say if you will only let me hold your bow."

But Apollo laughed, and taking Cupid's hand in his led him back to his mother.

Cupid was greatly disappointed and decided that if he could not have Apollo's bow and arrows he would get some for himself. He knew that

THE BABY SON OF VENUS

almost anything he wished for, Vulcan could make at his anvil, and so one day he asked for a bow like Apollo's, and a quiver of golden arrows.

Vulcan fashioned a little bow, perfect and smooth and slender, and a quiver full of the sharpest, lightest arrows.

Venus, who was watching, gave to these darts a power no large arrows had ever possessed. When any one was touched ever so lightly by one of the golden arrows, he at once fell in love with the first person he saw.

Cupid was so delighted with his bow and arrows that he played with them from morning until night.

"WHAT HAVE YOU TO DO WITH WARLIKE WEAPONS, SAUCY BOY?"

One day Apollo did not drive his chariot, but left it in the heavens behind the clouds.

"It is a good thing," he said, "for people to have some gray days." So he spent the day hunting through the forest.

In a little glade he came upon Cupid sitting on a mossy rock, playing with his bow and arrows. Apollo was much vexed to think that Cupid could handle so cleverly the same kind of weapons that he had used to kill the Python. He frowned, and spoke harshly to him.

"What have you to do with warlike weapons, saucy boy?" said Apollo. "Put them down and leave such things for grown people."

Cupid was hurt and angry. He had hoped Apollo would praise him for his skill, as Venus had done.

"Your arrows may kill the Python," said Cupid, "but mine shall wound you."

As he spoke he let fly an arrow, which struck Apollo so lightly it barely scratched him. Apollo laughed at him and walked on, not knowing what the wound really meant.

Soon he noticed a beautiful nymph gathering flowers in the forest. Her name was Daphne. Apollo had often seen her before, but she had never seemed so beautiful as now. He ran forward to speak to her. She saw him coming and was startled.

"Let me help you gather flowers," begged Apollo, but Daphne was so shy she ran away. Apollo wanted so much to be with her and talk to her that he ran after her.

Poor Daphne, terrified, ran faster and faster. When she was breathless and could run no more, she cried loudly to Peneus, the river god, for help.

Peneus was her father and, hearing his daughter's voice from

DAPHNE WAS SO SHY SHE RAN AWAY

far away, he thought she was in some terrible danger. Swiftly he sent his magic power over the forest, and to protect her changed her into a tree.

Daphne's feet clung to the earth and took root. She felt the rough bark creeping over her shoulders and limbs. From her arms sprang branches, and her hands were filled with leaves. When Apollo reached out his hand to touch her, the fair maiden had vanished. In her place stood a beautiful laurel tree.

"What have I done?" mourned Apollo.

He was so grieved and sad because he had brought this change on Daphne that he stayed by the tree all the afternoon, talking to it and begging Daphne to forgive him.

He asked for some of her laurel leaves that he might wear them on his head. Daphne shook her branches, and a little shower of leaves fell around Apollo. By this he knew that Daphne forgave him, and he gathered the leaves tenderly in his hands and wove them into a wreath.

Throwing aside a drooping wreath of flowers which he wore about his brow, Apollo placed the laurel on his head, where it remained forever fresh and green.

DIANA AND ACTAEON

~ 52 ~

In all the realm of King Cadmus there was no mortal hunter like young Prince Actaeon. The fiercest boars fell at the touch of his spear, so strong and sure was his thrust, and the dogs of his pack were not more swift in overtaking the deer than was Prince Actaeon himself.

Only one other excelled him in the hunt, and that was the goddess Diana, twin sister of Apollo. Followed by her nymphs, the fair goddess loved to roam the woods and mountains by day, hunting until the noon sun was high overhead, and the heat became too great for comfort.

Then the nymphs laid aside their bows and arrows, their spears and their mantles, to rest in a glade deep in the forest. Diana had chosen this home for herself, and it was held sacred for her use.

No mortal might go into the glade and live. The very air of this charmed place was so clear and sweet, so cool and fragrant, that mortals seemed warned before entering it. They knew that here among the trees in this fair grove was the resting place of some deity, and turned their steps away in reverence.

But one day when the noon heat was great, Actaeon, tired of the hunt, left his comrades and, following a little brook, wandered away into the depths of the wood, seeking a cool and restful spot. He came at last to the edge of Diana's glade and heard the splashing of water and the merry voices of the nymphs at play.

RAISING ONE OF THE URNS HIGH ABOVE HER HEAD, DIANA DASHED THE WATER IN ACTAEON'S FACE

Parting the branches of some laurel trees, he peeped through and saw a silvery fountain gushing from a rock, and a little pool of clear water where Diana and her nymphs were preparing to bathe. One nymph loosed the fillet which bound Diana's hair, so that it fell in shining waves over her bare shoulders and floated around her like a golden cloud. One untied the thongs of her sandals, while another laid aside her mantle and held ready fresh linen. Others busily drew water and filled great urns.

All these things Actaeon watched without thought of wrongdoing, until one of the nymphs happened to look toward the laurel trees and saw him peering out through the branches.

The nymph screamed, and ran to shield Diana from his curious gaze. The other maidens rushed also to screen the goddess, but it was too late!

A rosy color spread over Diana's cheeks and brow. Shame and anger were in her heart. She reached for her spear to kill Actaeon, but it lay far from her hand. Then she seized one of the urns and, raising it high above her head, dashed the water in Actaeon's face.

"Go, now," Diana cried, "and boast, if you can, of your boldness!"

Actaeon fell down on the bank of the little brook, and as he fell huge ears and branching antlers sprang from his head. His arms became hairy, and hoofs took the place of his hands and feet. Gazing in the clear water of the little brook, he saw only a frightened stag which bounded away through the woods.

Back toward his comrades Actaeon ran, but at sight of his dogs he felt a great fear and turned again into the forest. But the dogs had seen him and, leaping up at the sight of a deer, followed hard after poor Actaeon.

Never did he run so swiftly. Over rocks and hills and across streams he sped, with the fleetness of the wind, but still his dogs pursued him.

Now he thought sadly of how he himself had chased other deer, rejoicing to see them panting and weary. He remembered how often he had urged on his dogs and felt no pity.

As he ran Actaeon's heart beat wild and fast from fright and weariness, until at length, worn out, he fell to the earth, and the dogs overtook him.

A FRIGHTENED STAG BOUNDED AWAY THROUGH THE WOODS

His spirit passed from the body of the stag and slumbered ever after in the land of the shades.

Such was the harshness of the goddess Diana to mortals who were overbold.

PEGASUS AND BELLEROPHON

Pegasus was a wonderful winged horse which belonged to Minerva, the gray-eyed goddess who watched over heroes and gave wisdom and skill to all those who truly wished it.

Now it happened that after Minerva had caught and tamed Pegasus, the winged horse, she did not care to ride him herself, but knew no mortal who deserved to own him. So Minerva gave Pegasus to the nymphs to care for until she could find a youth brave enough and wise enough to ride him.

The nymphs were happy caring for Pegasus. They brushed him, combed his mane, and fed him, but they knew that by and by he would belong to a mortal master who would come and ride him away.

At last in Corinth there was born a little prince named Bellerophon. Glaucus, his father, had more skill in handling horses than any other man. As Bellerophon grew up, his father trained him and taught him all he knew, so that while Bellerophon was still very young he understood the ways of horses and learned to ride them.

All this time the winged horse was without a master.

When Bellerophon was sixteen he began to long for travel and adventure in other lands, so he set out to visit a neighboring king.

Many friends came to bid the gallant young man goodby and wish him well, but there was one, named Proetus, who pretended to be

Bellerophon's friend, but who really wished for him the worst that might happen. Proetus was jealous of Prince Bellerophon, and hoped that the young hero might not return from the journey.

WHILE STILL VERY YOUNG, BELLEROPHON UNDERSTOOD THE WAYS OF HORSES

It happened that Proetus was the son-in-law of Iobates, king of Lycia, and so, pretending friendship, Proetus gave Bellerophon a letter to carry to the king. Bellerophon, knowing nothing of the wicked words that were in this letter, put it carefully in the pocket of his tunic and rode gayly away.

When he reached Lycia, the home of Iobates, he found great sorrow in the land and all the people mourning. Each night a monster called the

Chimaera came down the valley and carried off women and children, sheep and oxen. The mountain where he lived was white with the bones of his victims.

Bellerophon rode through the mourning city and came to the palace of the king. He presented himself to Iobates and gave him the letter.

MINERVA, THE GRAY-EYED GODDESS

As the king read, his face darkened and he seemed troubled, for the letter asked that Bellerophon should be put to death. The king did not like to heed the request in this strange letter, yet he wished to please his son-in-law. He knew that to kill a guest would be a wicked deed and against the laws of kindness to a visitor, and might also bring war on him from the land where the young prince lived. So he decided to send Bellerophon to slay the Chimaera, thinking he never could come back alive.

Bellerophon was not the least bit afraid, because he longed for adventure, and his heart was filled with a great desire to overcome this dark and evil monster, free the kingdom from fear, and make the mourning people happy.

But before starting out he found the oldest and wisest man in the whole kingdom and asked his advice. This aged man was named Polyidus. When he saw that Bellerophon was young and full of courage, yet humble enough to ask help from some one older, Polyidus told him a secret which no one else in the kingdom knew.

He told him of Minerva's winged horse, which he had once seen drinking at a spring deep in the forest.

"If you sleep all night in Minerva's temple," said the old man, "and offer gifts at her altar, she may help you to find the horse."

Bellerophon went to the temple, and as he slept he dreamed that he saw Minerva, clad in silver armor, her gray eyes shining as if they held sparks of fire. Plumes of blue and rose and violet floated from her helmet. She carried a golden bridle in her hand and told Bellerophon how he might reach the well where Pegasus came to drink.

When Bellerophon awakened, he saw the golden bridle on the temple floor beside him, and knew Minerva really had visited him. Then with the bridle over his arm he set out on his journey through the forest. When he found the well, he hid himself among the bushes nearby to watch for the coming of the winged horse. At length Bellerophon saw the winged horse flying far up in the sky. Nearer

PEGASUS FLEW WILDLY OVER THE SEA AND THE MOUNTAINS

and nearer he wheeled until his silver feet touched the green grass beside the spring.

As Pegasus bent his head to drink, Bellerophon sprang from his hiding place and caught him by the mane. Before Pegasus knew what had happened, the golden bridle was slipped over his head, and Bellerophon had leaped to his back and was sitting between his outspread wings.

Pegasus rose into the air and darted wildly through the sky, now flying high among the clouds, now diving swiftly toward the earth. He reared and plunged, trying to shake Bellerophon from his back. He flew wildly over the sea and the mountains all the way to Africa and back. He flew over Thebes and over Corinth, and people looking up into the sky thought they saw some strange bird passing overhead.

But Bellerophon understood how to handle fierce horses, for he remembered the things his father had taught him. At last Pegasus knew he had found his master and, tired and panting, sank down to the grass beside the well.

After Pegasus had rested, Bellerophon armed himself with a long spear and rode toward the mountain where dwelt the Chimaera.

There on a ledge of rock outside his cave the monster lay basking in the sunlight. He was partly like a lion and partly like a dragon. He lay with his lion's head resting between his paws and his long green tail, like that of a lizard, curled around him.

Bellerophon rode his horse as near as he dared to the ledge on which the dragon lay, then raised his spear to strike at the Chimaera,

WITH ONE STRONG THRUST, BELLEROPHON SENT HIS SPEAR THROUGH THE HEART OF THE CHIMAERA

but the great beast blew out clouds of smoke and fire, and Pegasus drew back in terror.

As the monster drew in his breath for another puff, Bellerophon rode close to the ledge and with one strong thrust sent his spear through the heart of the Chimaera.

When the young prince came back to the palace, riding the winged horse and carrying the head of the dreadful Chimaera, there was wild rejoicing in Lycia. Everyone admired and praised Bellerophon, and crowded around the wonderful horse, amazed at his wings and his silver feet.

The young daughter of King Iobates, who came out on the portico of the palace to see the hero and his horse, fell in love with Bellerophon the moment she saw the young warrior sitting so proudly between the white wings of Pegasus. King Iobates led her to Bellerophon and gave her to him for his bride.

For a long time they were happy together. Bellerophon and Pegasus went on many adventures, and when Iobates died Bellerophon became king.

At last one day Bellerophon thought of a most daring adventure. He decided he would try to ride Pegasus to Mount Olympus and visit the gods.

Minerva appeared and warned him that the gods would be angry, but he mounted his horse and rose high into the clouds, urging Pegasus up toward the summit of Mount Olympus.

Jupiter looked down and, seeing the horse approaching, was angry to think that any mortal should dare approach the home of the gods. He caused a gadfly to light on Pegasus and sting his neck and his shoulders and his nose.

Pegasus was so startled by this that at once he reared and wheeled among the clouds, leaping wildly in the air, and Bellerophon was thrown from his back and dropped down to earth.

Minerva, causing him to land where the ground was soft, spared his life, but as long as he lived Bellerophon wandered, crippled and lonely, seeking all over the earth for his wonderful winged horse.

But Pegasus never again returned to him.

CUPID AND PSYCHE

Once there lived in Greece a blue-eyed princess named Psyche. She was so fair, so beautiful, that strangers came from far-away countries to look at her and scatter roses in her path. When she smiled, even the immortals were delighted as they watched her from the heights of Mount Olympus.

Only one grew angry when Psyche was praised. Venus, the goddess of beauty, looked down at her temples on the earth and saw that they were empty. The young men who should have brought garlands for her altars were casting chaplets of roses at Psyche's feet and singing hymns of praise to her. So Venus called her son Cupid and sent him to wound Psyche with one of his golden arrows.

Cupid sharpened his weapons as his mother bade him, flew down to the palace where Psyche lay asleep, and lightly touched his golden arrow to her side. At once Psyche awoke and turned her eyes toward Cupid, although she could not see him, for he was invisible.

She was so wonderfully fair that Cupid's heart beat wildly as he bent over her, and a weakness came over him such as he had never felt before. His hand slipped, and he wounded himself with his own arrow. That moment Cupid fell in love with Psyche, a mortal maiden.

Troubled and bewildered, he flew back to Olympus and praised the lovely Psyche to his mother. Now Venus was more angry with Psyche

AS SHE LAY ASLEEP, CUPID LIGHTLY TOUCHED HIS GOLDEN ARROW TO PSYCHE'S SIDE

than before. By her arts she turned all of Psyche's lovers away from her, and she forbade Cupid ever to enter the palace of the blue-eyed princess or to look upon her again.

Soon Psyche's elder sisters were married to great princes, but no lover sought Psyche, although she grew more and more lovely. At length her parents, feeling sure that the gods were angry, journeyed to the temple of Apollo to seek advice of the oracle.

"The maiden is to be the bride of an immortal lover," the oracle replied, "a monster of such power that neither gods nor men can resist him. He awaits her on the top of the mountain."

This answer filled the king and queen and all their people with terror, but Psyche robed herself in her most beautiful garments and, followed by her parents and friends, ascended the mountain. At the top they bade her good-by and left her there alone.

While Psyche stood on the mountain top, weeping and trembling with fright, Zephyr, the west wind, lifted her gently in his arms and carried her to a flowery valley below. Nearby in a grove of tall and stately trees she saw a wonderful white palace, and in an open place fountains played amid blossoming branches. As she drew nearer to the palace she knew it was the home of an immortal, so great was its splendor. Golden pillars supported the high-arched roof, and paintings and sculpture ornamented the walls.

As she walked through the lovely rooms a voice all sweetness and gentleness spoke to her, "Fair Princess, all that you behold is yours. Command us, we are your servants." Filled with wonder and delight, Psyche looked about in all directions, but saw no one. The voice continued, "Here is your chamber, and your bed of down; here is your bath, and in the adjoining alcove there is food."

Psyche bathed, and put on the lovely garments prepared for her, then seated herself on a chair of carved ivory. At once there floated to its place before her a table covered with golden dishes and with the finest food. Although she could see no one, invisible hands served her, and unseen musicians played on lutes and sang to her.

For a long time Psyche did not see the master of the palace. He visited her only in the nighttime, going away before morning dawned, but his voice was gentle and tender, not at all like that of a monster. Psyche sometimes begged him to stay through the day, but always he replied, "If you beheld my face, perhaps you would fear me, perhaps adore me, but I would rather you should love me as an equal than adore me as a god."

ZEPHYR, THE WEST WIND, LIFTED HER GENTLY IN HIS ARMS AND
CARRIED HER TO A FLOWERY VALLEY

Psyche next begged her husband that her sisters might visit her. Although Cupid knew there would be trouble if they entered his home, he yielded to Psyche's pleading, and Zephyr was sent to bring them across the mountain and down to the enchanted valley. At first they were happy to see their young sister and to find her safe, but soon, seeing all the

"LOVE CANNOT DWELL WITH SUSPICION," CUPID SAID SADLY

splendor in Psyche's palace, envy sprang up in their hearts. They questioned her rudely concerning her husband.

"Is he not some dreadful monster," they asked, "some dragon, who will at length devour you? Remember what the oracle said!"

Before their visit was over they begged Psyche to look at Cupid as he lay asleep. They urged her to carry a lamp and a great knife, so that she might cut off his head if he were indeed a dragon. Psyche promised to do so, and her sisters departed.

Psyche hid the lamp and knife where she could find them quickly. At midnight, when her lord was sleeping, she arose, lit her lamp, and bent over his couch. The light showed her, not a dragon nor a monster, but a youth more beautiful than any she had ever seen, with golden curls falling over his pillow, and white wings gleaming softly, like pearl and crystal.

As she turned to put out the lamp a drop of burning oil fell upon his shoulder. Cupid awoke and, looking at her sorrowfully, spread his shining wings and flew out of the window. Psyche held wide her arms and, standing on the ledge of the window, tried to follow him. But Zephyr did not receive her, and she fell.

For an instant Cupid turned back to her. "Love cannot dwell with suspicion," he said sadly, and flew away.

As Psyche lay weeping, the palace and gardens and fountains vanished, and she found herself again in her own land. Sadly she went to the palace and told her sisters what had happened. She would not stay with her sisters, but wandered away to seek her beloved. Day and night, without food or rest, she journeyed over the wildest mountains. At last she saw a beautiful temple gleaming on a hill.

"Perhaps he is there," she thought, and climbed breathlessly to the hilltop. She entered the temple. Before the altar of Ceres she saw sheaves of barley, ears of corn, piles of grain, and sickles and rakes thrown down in careless disorder by the tired harvesters.

Psyche stooped and carefully piled the grain and the sheaves of barley. She gathered the sickles and rakes and placed them on the steps of the temple, where the reapers might find them in the morning. Then, when she had swept the floor, she seated herself to rest.

Ceres, the goddess of this temple, was pleased at Psyche's service, and advised her to go at once to Venus, offer to serve her, and beg for pity and forgiveness. When Psyche reached the court of Venus, she knelt before the goddess and promised to serve her in whatever way Venus might wish if only she might be allowed to see Cupid and finally be forever near him. Venus was still angry with Psyche, so she set her the most difficult tasks she could find.

She led Psyche to a storehouse where there were great piles of wheat, barley, millet, lentils, and beans, which Venus kept for her doves.

"First sort these grains," said Venus. "Put each kind in a separate bag, and finish the task by nightfall."

Psyche sat down on the floor of the storeroom and gazed hopelessly at the piles of grain. She knew she could not finish the task before evening, nor even if she toiled for many days. But Cupid, who still loved her, had been listening, and he now sent those tireless little workers, the ants, to help. They came marching from their hills in long black lines and crawled up on the piles of grain. Then, each carrying one kernel at a time, they patiently sorted the piles and filled the bags before evening.

When Venus returned she found everything in order. But when she saw that Psyche's task was completed, she was more angry than ever, for

VENUS COMMANDED PSYCHE TO GO TO THE REALM OF PROSERPINA AND PLUTO

she felt sure that Cupid had helped her. Throwing a piece of black bread to Psyche for her supper, she left her.

The next morning Venus sent Psyche to bring a sample of golden wool from each of the sheep in a flock that fed across a nearby river. As Psyche stood on the river bank wondering how she might cross, the river god bade the rushes and reeds murmur softly and tell her she must not try to cross in the morning, nor venture among the angry rams until the noon shadows lay deep and the sheep went to rest in the shade.

Psyche waited on the river bank until noontime, when the sheep were drowsing in the shade, and then crossed safely over. She gathered the golden fleece from the bushes where it was clinging, and carried it back to Venus. But Venus gave her no praise, only another crust for her supper.

The third day Venus commanded Psyche to go to the realm of Proserpina and Pluto, and say to Proserpina, "My mistress Venus begs you to send her a little of your beauty, for in caring for her wounded son she has lost some of her own."

CHARON FERRIED PSYCHE ACROSS THE DARK WATER

Now Psyche was more hopeless than ever, for she was sure she never could travel on foot to Erebus, where Proserpina dwelt. But when she was most downhearted a friendly voice explained to her how she might safely pass the dangers on her way. It told her how to weave a charm about

Cerberus, the three-headed dog, and how to prevail on Charon, the aged boatman of the river Styx, to row her across the stream and back again. It warned her especially not to open the jar in which she was to carry the precious beauty.

The voice reminded her of Cupid, whom she had lost. It was tender, like the voice of her lover, and gentle. So courage came into her heart, and she set forth, carrying a golden jar in her hands. She walked through a dark cave and on through a narrow passageway, dripping with water, until she came to a wider entrance where Cerberus, wit h his three great heads, barked fiercely and shook the earth with his growls. Trembling, she kept her face toward him, talking gently to him as she drew nearer.

His barking ceased, and his growling grew fainter and fainter. When she reached him he lay down and thumped the ground with his tail, just as the friendly dogs of the earth always did when Psyche passed by them.

At the river Styx the aged boatman took her hand and led her to the boat. He ferried her across the dark water, and Psyche went on her way to Proserpina's throne, where she delivered the message from Venus.

When Proserpina had filled the golden jar, Psyche again returned and crossed the river with Charon. Passing the dreadful Cerberus, she at last found herself outside the cave in the sunshine. As she rested on a grassy bank she looked longingly at the little jar.

"What harm can it do," Psyche thought, "if I just peep in and take a tiny bit of the beauty for myself, so that when Cupid again sees me I shall be even more lovely?"

So she took off the lid, and at once up into her face flew clouds of strange fragrance. She could not see the jar or even the grass around her, but fell back asleep. Cupid, still invisible, had been waiting and watching at the entrance of the cavern for her return. He flew to her side, and gathering the clouds of sleepy magic he placed them again in the jar and wakened Psyche.

"Again," he said, "you have almost perished because of your curiosity."

Psyche was so happy to be with Cupid that she would have forgotten to finish her errand. But Cupid knew that Venus must be obeyed, and he sent Psyche on with the jar while he himself flew to Jupiter and begged that Psyche might be made immortal so that she might stay with him forever.

Jupiter granted Cupid's plea, and sent Mercury, messenger of the gods, to carry Psyche to Mount Olympus, where the gods were waiting to welcome her.

A glorious haze of light, as many-colored as a rainbow, hid the throne of Jupiter from Psyche's sight, for being mortal she might not look on the ruler of the gods.

Hebe, the cupbearer of the immortals, advanced to meet her, carrying in her hand a goblet of ambrosia, which she gave to Psyche.

HEBE, THE CUPBEARER OF THE GODS

The fragrant liquid not only refreshed Psyche but bestowed upon her the gift of immortality. Immediately after she had emptied the goblet her weariness fell from her, her body felt new strength, her heart was filled with new gladness, and her face and form appeared more lovely than ever.

The haze of light rolled away from Jupiter's throne, and Psyche beheld the ruler of the gods. Kneeling before him, she gave him humble thanks.

Venus, feeling forgiveness in her heart, now came forward to embrace Psyche and give her to Cupid for his bride.

Ever after, on the sunny summit of Mount Olympus, Cupid and Psyche lived together in happiness.

CIRCE AND ULYSSES

There was once a beautiful enchantress named Circe. Her palace stood in a grove on the island of Eaea. Here she lived alone and spent her time in studying magic.

THE GREAT ULYSSES

She learned all sorts of sorcery and tricks, and became so clever that she could turn men into whatever beasts she liked.

When strangers landed on her island, she changed them into lions and wolves and pigs. Her garden was full of enchanted animals, which wandered back and forth, remembering that they were really men.

They longed to speak, but could only grunt or growl. Her pig sties were crowded. But in all her palace there was no friend or servant, or any living person to keep her company.

One day a ship dropped anchor in the bay, and a band of sailors came wading ashore for water. Their leader was the great Ulysses. He was on his voyage home to Ithaca, and had been through many dangers and hardships. His men were very hungry, and their clothes were ragged and travel-stained.

Eurylochus led his men through the woods toward the smoke, and at last they saw a beautiful palace, half hidden by trees. The columns gleamed like white marble, and a fountain sprayed into the air. The men were sure they would be received with kindness in so fair a palace.

But as they came still nearer, they were terrified to see wild animals roaming through the gardens. There were lions and tigers and wolves walking sleepily back and forth among the trees. Eurylochus and his comrades drew back and hid themselves where they could watch. They noticed that the animals were drowsy and quiet. Soon the men gathered courage to steal toward the palace.

The beasts did not leap at them, or roar, but made low gentle sounds, and crowded around Eurylochus. They lay on the ground at his feet, and tried to lick his hands. He thought he saw a pleading look in their eyes. Indeed, he had never before seen such eyes in any animals. They were like the eyes of men in trouble.

He patted their heads and walked on toward the entrance of the palace, where he heard music and the sound of singing.

He called aloud, and a lovely woman, veiled in many garments, came floating toward him. Her thin scarfs fluttered in the soft wind, and her voice, as she invited the strangers to enter, was low and sweet.

They crowded into the palace, delighted at her welcome, but Eurylochus looked into her eyes and saw that they were small and cruel. He felt he would rather stay outside with the animals than follow her inside the huge door.

As the doors clanged together behind his comrades, the beasts uttered such mournful sounds that Eurylochus hid himself beside one of the windows. There he could see what happened in the palace and help his friends if they fell into danger.

He saw them seated at a great banqueting table, with warm food and fruit before them and all manner of sweet things. While they ate, the air was filled with perfume and soft music. Eurylochus was very hungry himself, and the sight of the food almost made him wish that he had entered with his companions.

When the men had finished, they stretched themselves on the stone benches to rest, or sat sleepily in their chairs. Then their hostess took a little ivory wand in her hand and touched them very lightly, one by one. At once long ears began to spring from their heads, and their bodies were covered with bristles. Hoofs took the place of their hands and feet, and they fell to the floor on all fours.

CIRCE TOOK AN IVORY WAND IN HER HAND AND TOUCHED THE MEN ONE BY ONE

Before Eurylochus knew what was happening, his comrades had vanished, and in their stead a dozen grunting pigs waddled around the banquet hall.

Then he knew that their lovely hostess was Circe, the enchantress. He understood why the lions and tigers had looked at him so sadly, and had made such mournful sounds when the doors had closed behind his friends.

As he watched, he saw Circe lead her pigs out of the palace and shut them in a dirty sty. She threw them a bagful of acorns, and laughed at them as they crowded to the fence, looking up at her pleadingly.

Eurylochus ran back to the ship and told the others what had happened. Ulysses at once started out to rescue his men, depending only upon his sword. As he hurried through the woods, the god Mercury appeared to him.

"However brave you may be," said the god, "your sword will not overcome the magic of Circe. But if you carry this sprig of green in your hand, it will keep you safe from her sorcery."

He put a branch of a plant called Moly into the hand of Ulysses, and vanished. Still holding the green sprig, Ulysses entered the palace garden. The beasts crowded close around him and followed him to the door.

Circe herself came to meet him, much pleased to have another victim as handsome and strong as Ulysses.

She seated him at the banquet table, and smiled as she watched him eat, thinking what a fine large boar he would make. But when she touched him with her wand, the power of the little plant turned her magic aside.

Ulysses did not fall to the floor, nor waddle away grunting. Instead he drew his sword and rushed at her, commanding her to release his friends.

Circe was so frightened that she knelt before him and begged him to spare her. She promised to free all her prisoners, even the lions and wolves in the garden. She agreed to help Ulysses on his journey, and to provide food and water for him to carry away in his ship.

She ran to the pig sties and as she touched each one of the boars, it changed again into its own form.

The beasts in the garden became men, and spoke to one another once more in words instead of in growls. They thought only of returning to their own homes and friends, and began to make plans for their journey.

Circe kept her promise and helped Ulysses on his voyage. She provided him with all manner of good things, and warned him of dangers which he might meet on the sea.

Seeing that the clothes of Ulysses and his friends were travel-stained and worn, she gave them beautiful robes from her own chests. She made a new sail for their boat, and was so busy that for the time she forgot her evil arts of magic.

At last everything was ready for Ulysses' departure.

The ship with its white sail lay floating near the shore. The men put

CIRCE KNELT BEFORE ULYSSES AND BEGGED HIM TO SPARE HER

on their fresh robes. Then they carried on board jugs of water and wine, sacks of meal, smoked meat, and all the things that they might need on the voyage.

The men seized the oars in their hands. The sail filled with wind, and Ulysses sped away from the island of Circe, favored by her help, toward Ithaca, his home.

POMONA AND VERTUMNUS

omona was a nymph who cared for the fruit-bearing trees of the orchards. While her sisters watched over the trees of the forests, Pomona worked among her apple trees, her pear trees, and her

THE NYMPH POMONA

vines. She pruned and tended them from dawn until dark. She led little streams to water their roots, and cut off the long useless shoots.

She trained the grape vines to climb on the trunks of elm trees, so that they spread among the branches until the elms looked as though they were full of blue and amber grapes.

Many lovers came wooing Pomona, the fauns and satyrs and even the god Pan. His legs were like a goat's, but he played such music on his pipes that the nymphs would have no one else to play for their dancing.

Pomona would not think of romance or of wedding anyone. She cared only for her garden and her fruit trees. She loaded her suitors with fruit and sent them all away.

The country people around her, who had gardens of their own, were a great trouble to Pomona. They tried to steal her fruit, and cut shoots from her trees to graft on their own. So she built a high wall around her garden and allowed no suitors or idle country folk to enter through the little gate. After the wall was built her lovers grew discouraged, except one who loved her best of all.

His name was Vertumnus, and he was the god of the changing seasons. He possessed the power of taking any form he wished. Sometimes he pretended to be a reaper, and came to Pomona's gate with a basket of corn to sell. At other times he would carry a pruning hook, and offer to climb the highest trees and to trim the branches which Pomona could not reach. On other days he dressed like a fisherman, and brought her little spotted trout from the streams. In these ways he was allowed to come in through the gate and visit Pomona each day, until he grew to love her more than ever.

Once he came as an aged woman, who wore a dark cloak and asked

PAN'S LEGS WERE LIKE A GOAT'S, BUT HE PLAYED SUCH MUSIC THAT THE
NYMPHS WOULD HAVE NO ONE ELSE TO PLAY FOR THEIR DANCING

permission to enter the garden and see the fruit. Pomona smiled, and
swung the gate wide open. She led the old woman to a grassy bank, and
helped her to seat herself beneath a tree. She gathered her largest and
reddest apples and offered them to her visitor.

"Do you tend this garden all alone?" asked the woman. "What!

Have you not chosen a suitor? Do you mean to live alone like this forever?"

Pomona smiled and said that she cared more for her garden than for any youth, and that she liked to live alone. Then the aged stranger pointed to an elm tree on which Pomona had trained her grapes.

"If yonder vine were not twined around the elm," she said, "it would lie on the ground. The sun could never reach the grapes to ripen them and make them grow. You are like the vine, and I will tell you of someone who is like the elm."

The old woman then began to praise Vertumnus.

"No one is stronger, or kinder, or more beautiful than he, and like yourself, he delights in gardening."

She talked so long of this suitor that at length Pomona became interested and almost wished to see him.

Then the old woman craftily began to tell Pomona the story of Anaxarete: how that noble lady scorned her lovers and would marry no one, until at last, in despair, the most ardent of them, named Iphis, killed himself for love of her, and Anaxarete was turned to stone as a punishment for her hardness.

Then, with a laugh, the old woman added, "Beware lest your own coldness bring you a like fate!"

As she spoke her dark cloak fell from her, her wrinkles vanished, her bent shoulders straightened, and Vertumnus himself stood before Pomona.

POMONA GATHERED HER LARGEST AND REDDEST APPLES AND OFFERED THEM TO HER VISITOR

When he spoke, it was in a voice very different from that of the old woman. Pomona thought it more beautiful than any voice she had ever heard.

As she led him around the garden, Pomona said, "You are indeed like the elm tree, and I would rather be like the vine than like the noble lady Anaxarete."

PERSEUS AND ANDROMEDA

~ 91 ~

A fisherman was tending his nets one morning on the coast of Seriphus when he noticed something floating far out on the water. He rowed out and found a great wooden chest, which he towed to shore. When the fisherman pried up the heavy cover, he found inside the chest a beautiful princess with a little baby clasped in her arms.

She had been shut in the chest for so many hours, floating over the sea, that she could not stand for weakness. So the fisherman lifted both baby and mother in his arms and carried them to the King.

A FISHERMAN WAS TENDING HIS NETS ON THE COAST OF SERIPHUS

THE FISHERMAN FOUND INSIDE THE CHEST A BEAUTIFUL PRINCESS WITH A LITTLE BABY CLASPED IN HER ARMS

Everyone in the palace was greatly surprised to see the strange princess and her baby. King Polydectes ordered food and wine for the mother, and the women of the palace bathed the baby and clothed him in fresh linen.

When the princess had eaten and felt refreshed, she told the King that her name was Danae and that her baby was Perseus, the little son of Jupiter. She told him that her father, King Acrisius of Argos, had shut them in the chest and set them afloat on the sea because he had heard from an oracle that some day the baby Perseus would grow up and cause his death.

Polydectes was delighted to have Danae stay in the palace, and for a long time he took care of her and her little son. But as Perseus grew up, Polydectes cared less for him, and finally began to wish that Perseus would go away.

So Polydectes sent him on a dangerous journey, to kill the gorgon Medusa, whose cavern was far away in the wilderness. Medusa's head was so terrible to see that no one could look at her without being turned into stone from sheer horror.

Perseus was glad to be sent on this adventure. He armed himself well and set out bravely toward the wilderness where Medusa dwelt.

Minerva, the goddess who watches over heroes, saw him depart, and feared that he could not succeed without the help of the gods. Perseus wore a sword and carried a shield and his sandals were light and strong, but Minerva knew that he would need weapons and armor more powerful than mortal sword or shield, and sandals swifter than his leathern ones.

Therefore she called upon Mercury, who brought his winged sandals of silver. Pluto, god of Erebus, lent his plumed helmet, which would make the wearer invisible.

Minerva, herself, gave her shield, which nothing could pierce or shatter.

When Perseus strapped the winged sandals on his feet he felt himself rise with a strange lightness. When the helmet touched his head, he became invisible. With the strong and beautiful shield in his hand he

MERCURY BROUGHT HIS WINGED SANDALS, PLUTO LENT HIS PLUMED HELMET, AND
MINERVA HERSELF GAVE HER SHIELD

set out, as swiftly as Mercury himself, flying through the air over tree tops and temples, toward the cavern of the Graeae.

He knew that these three aged sisters, the Graeae, were exceedingly wise, as wise as they were old, and that if they wished they could tell him where to find Medusa.

As he drew near their cavern, he could hear them singing a mournful song, and, as he peered into the gloomy depths, he saw them rocking back and forth as they sang. They were bent and wrinkled and blind, except for one movable eye which they shared among them. They passed it back and forth as each took her turn at seeing. Their long white hair hung wild and loose on their shoulders.

MEDUSA'S HEAD WAS TERRIBLE TO SEE

As Perseus watched, one of them plucked the eye from her forehead and passed it to the sister next to her. For a moment she groped, reaching out for her sister's hand. Instantly, when all the Graeae were in darkness, Perseus sprang into the cavern and snatched the eye as it passed between their fingers.

For a moment there was terrible confusion, for each sister thought one of the others was hiding it. Then Perseus spoke to them and they knew that a stranger had stolen their eye. They stumbled around the cavern, blindly holding out their hands to find him, wailing and pleading all the time.

Perseus was sorry for them, but he did not intend to return their eye until they told him where to find the Gorgon. The Graeae were willing to do anything to have their eye again, and so they agreed to give Perseus all the help they could. They told him exactly in which direction he must go, and just how to find the cavern of Medusa.

Perseus returned their eye and thanked them. Then, swiftly, he flew to the home of Medusa.

Perseus found the entrance to her cave exactly where the Graeae had told him. On every side stood figures of stone, their faces turned toward the cavern. They wore such an expression of terror that Perseus was careful to keep his face turned away, lest he should see Medusa.

From inside the cave he could hear strange noises, as of someone walking about and complaining. He heard the whispering sound made by the hissing of the serpents which formed Medusa's hair.

Hiding himself behind one of the stone images he waited until nightfall, then stole up quietly and found the spot where Medusa slept. Although he kept his head turned aside, he could see her reflection in the brightness of his shield.

Bending over, Perseus cut off the Gorgon's head, and carrying it with him hurried to the entrance of the cave. He rose into the air, and flew over the sea and over Africa. As he passed, some drops of the

Gorgon's blood fell on the sands of the African desert and immediately changed into poisonous serpents.

At length Perseus came to the realm of a king named Atlas. When he asked for food and rest, Atlas refused him and drove him from the palace doors.

Perseus uncovered the head of Medusa and raised it in front of Atlas. As soon as the King beheld it, he was turned to stone. As Perseus watched, Atlas grew larger and larger. His hips formed the slopes of a mighty mountain; his hair and beard became forests, and thrusting his head high among the stars, he was forced to receive the weight of the sky on his shoulders. Forever after he was doomed to bear that burden.

Perseus flew on until he came to the land of Ethiopia. Here he noticed a group of people on the shore, wringing their hands and weeping. Chained to a nearby rock he saw a maiden who kept her face turned toward the sea. She seemed to be expecting something to approach, from across the water.

Perseus floated down and, as he came near her, he found that she was the loveliest maiden he had ever beheld. He took off his invisible helmet and spoke to her thus:

"O Virgin, undeserving of those chains, tell me, I beseech you, your name and the name of your country, and why you are thus bound."

Replying, the maiden told Perseus that she was Andromeda, Princess of Ethiopia. She was bound to the rock to await the coming of a sea-dragon which would devour her because the gods of the sea were angry with her mother.

Being beautiful and proud of her charms, the Queen of Ethiopia had boasted that she was lovelier than the sea nymphs. Neptune's daughters were angry at this boast, and as a punishment they sent a dreadful sea-dragon to carry off the fairest youths and maidens that lived in the land.

At last the King and Queen were warned by the gods that they must chain their own daughter to a rock so that the dragon might be given the loveliest maiden in all the kingdom. Then, said the oracle, the dragon would be satisfied and would return to the depths of the sea from which he had come.

Even as Andromeda was telling these things to Perseus they heard a roaring sound that came from the sea. As they looked up a huge green monster swam swiftly across the water, throwing great fountains of spray toward the heavens.

Perseus sprang into the air. As the dragon came near, he darted downward like an eagle and buried his sword in the serpent's shoulder. Such a fight followed that Andromeda covered her eyes in terror.

The monster lashed his tail to the right and to the left, and in his fury split great rocks. Again and again Perseus rose into the air and swooped down upon him, wounding him until at last he lay still, partly in the water and partly on shore, his head and body stretched on the rocks and the sand, his tail floating far out on the sea.

Perseus unbound the Princess, and the King and Queen gave a great banquet in his honor. Then they allowed him to marry Andromeda and carry her back to his own land.

AS THE DRAGON CAME NEAR, PERSEUS DARTED DOWNWARD LIKE AN EAGLE

Perseus returned the helmet to Pluto, the shield to Minerva, and the winged sandals to Mercury, and forever after lived happily with Andromeda.

The oracle which declared that Perseus would cause the death of King Acrisius spoke truly. For one day, after Perseus had returned to his own land, he was playing with the discus and threw it in a course too curved. With a flash of light like that of a swinging sword, the sharp discus flew beyond the limits of the field and struck the King a mortal blow. Thus the words of the ancient oracle came true.

THE PYGMIES AND THE CRANES

In a valley in Africa, surrounded by high mountains and wide deserts, there once lived a race of very little people called Pygmies. The tallest man among them was no larger than a year-old baby.

They had little villages of houses just big enough for them to stand up in. They had tiny chariots in which to ride. Their bowls and dishes were the size of those which little girls use for dolls' tea parties.

They ate fruit and berries and small fish which the Pygmy fishermen caught in the river in nets made of goat's hair.

Some wore tunics of mole and squirrel fur, while others had small garments made by the Pygmy women from flax which they had spun and woven.

Altogether they were very happy little people, except only at one time of year, when the cold and the snow drove the cranes from northern countries, and sent them south.

These great long-billed birds liked to fly to Africa and spend the winter where the weather was warm and pleasant.

Wherever they alighted, they ate all the fruit from the trees and the berries from the bushes. They ruined the cornfields and trampled the flax.

The Pygmies did not want the cranes to stop in their valley or on the hills around them. So the little men armed themselves with clubs and stones, and tried to drive the great birds away.

Each year many of the cranes were killed, yet every season as the birds flew south they continued to stop at the Pygmies' valley and steal grain and fruit from their fields and gardens. Sometimes they even carried away the Pygmy babies.

Now it happened that in the valley next to that of the Pygmies there

THE PYGMIES ARMED THEMSELVES AND TRIED TO DRIVE THE GREAT BIRDS AWAY

SOMETIMES THE CRANES EVEN CARRIED AWAY THE PYGMY BABIES

lived a giant named Antaeus. He was the little people's friend and helped them in their war against the cranes.

Antaeus was the son of Neptune and the Earth. His power was unconquerable so long as his feet touched the ground, for the strength of the Earth seemed to flow into his body.

Hercules, hearing of Antaeus, wished to try his strength, and came to Africa to wrestle with the giant.

When the Pygmies learned that Hercules had come to fight with their friend, they climbed the hill overlooking Antaeus' valley, and hid themselves behind trees to watch.

Hercules challenged the giant and they locked their mighty arms around each other. Over and over they rolled, crashing down trees and scattering rocks as they wrestled. But the struggle did not tire Antaeus, for his feet still touched the earth.

At last Hercules realized that Antaeus got his strength from Mother Earth. He lifted him high in the air, and the magic strength of Antaeus left him. He grew limp and weak and lifeless, so Hercules won the fight. Tired out, he lay down to rest.

The Pygmies grieved to see Antaeus overcome. They stole down from the hilltop and would have done harm to Hercules as he lay asleep. They formed in battle line, seized their tiny spears and shields, and marched upon him, but Hercules awakened at the first prick of their little spears, and laughed at them as they charged against him and beat upon his legs.

He gathered a few of them in his arms and carried them back to Greece, intending to give them to the children of his king.

At first the poor little Pygmies were badly frightened. On the journey, Hercules carried them carefully in a pouch made of his lion's skin cloak. He let them keep their heads out, that they might see the lands through which they passed. He fed them honey and fruit, and soon the Pygmies grew fond of him, and seemed quite happy and contented.

When he reached his own land he gave them to the children of King Eurystheus for pets.

We do not know what happened to the strange little people in their new home, but it is certain that they must have enjoyed all the new and wonderful sights, and the children of King Eurystheus must have found great happiness in their new friends.

It is very likely that the little princesses made them garments of linen and silk, and fed them from the daintiest of their dishes.

The Pygmies may have sat with them at lessons, and learned much wisdom.

It is pleasant to hope that one day, wise and traveled and experienced beyond any of their race, they returned to Africa to their own people, and shared with them the wonders they had seen in Greece.

TRANSFORMATIONS

The gods were very fond of transforming, or changing, the shape of things. They loved to come down to earth, disguised in different ways, and walk around and listen to everything that went on.

When a mortal offended them, they changed him into something unpleasant. But often when the gods saw a man in danger, they helped him to escape by changing him into a tree or an animal. The punishments of the gods were severe. Sometimes, for even a little thing such as breaking the branches of a tree, they would imprison a mortal forever.

DRYOPE

Dryope was a beautiful Greek woman whom the gods punished harshly. One day Dryope and her sister went walking to gather flowers along the river. Dryope carried her baby boy in her arms, and beside them ran Iole, her sister, gathering myrtle and violets, never guessing what would happen before they returned.

Soon Dryope grew tired carrying her baby, and sat down to rest on a grassy bank beside the water. Near her a lovely lotus tree drooped its branches over the water, and the baby reached his hands toward the purple flowers.

WHEN HE WAS NO LONGER A BABY, DRYOPE'S SON STILL CAME TO
THE LOTUS TREE

Dryope picked some of the clusters and gave them to the baby, and Iole had just reached her hand to gather another cluster when they noticed purple drops falling from the broken stems.

Just then an aged fagot-gatherer came by, and raising his hands in horror, said that in this tree lived the nymph Lotis. They had broken the branches and the nymph would die. Surely the gods would send a terrible punishment.

As he spoke, Dryope felt a strange stiffness come into her feet, and bark began to creep upwards over her body.

Branches sprang from her two arms, and she could no longer fold them around the baby, who fell tumbling to the grass.

Iole clung to her sister as if she would hold back the brown bark that crept over her.

Soon a young lotus tree stood in Dryope's place. Only her face remained among the branches and looked sadly down on her baby and her sister.

She begged that Iole would bring the baby every day to play under the tree, and charged her especially to teach him never to break a branch or to pick a flower. As she spoke the leaves spread over her face, and Dryope was completely hidden by the tree.

To be shut up like this forever seems terrible, but no doubt Dryope soon began to feel like the nymphs who chose trees for their dwellings.

When the sun came up each morning and shone on her leaves, she must have felt a comforting warmth. In midsummer, she must have been glad when the rain came dropping on her boughs. And how happy and proud must Dryope have felt in blossom time, when every one of her boughs hung heavy with white and purple flowers!

Each day her little boy was carried to the river bank to talk with his mother in the lotus tree, and her branches would reach down and touch him with a caress.

When he was no longer a baby, her son still came to the tre e. Even when he grew up, he sat in its shade to rest and to tell his mother about his happiness, his troubles, and his victories.

CLYTIE

Sometimes the gods changed people into other forms out of kindness. There was the water nymph Clytie, who once saw Apollo as, with his sister Diana, he went hunting through the forest.

Apollo was the most beautiful of all the gods. Clytie had never seen anyone so splendid or so glorious. She loved him at once. But Apollo hurried by without even noticing her as she stood beside her little stream.

Clytie followed him, hoping that he would speak to her. But the hunting party soon reached the edge of the wood, and Apollo rose in a pale cloud, and disappeared toward the East.

The sky was gray, and there had been no sunshine all forenoon because Apollo, hunting on earth, had not driven his chariot across the heavens.

Clytie watched the gray sky longingly. In a little while the mist began to scatter, and a pale yellow glow ran around the curving edges of the clouds. Then with a burst of light, the chariot of the sun appeared, midway on its course.

"That is his chariot," sighed poor Clytie, and sat down on the ground to watch it.

All afternoon she watched it. Every day for nine days she sat in the same place, looking upward and longing for Apollo to come to earth that she might see his face.

FOR NINE DAYS CLYTIE SAT IN THE SAME PLACE LOOKING UPWARD

She forgot to eat and grew thinner and thinner.

At last the gods were sorry for her and changed her into a great golden sunflower. Her seeds spread over the earth and grew. Wherever the sun shone, they raised their yellow heads to its light and turned, now east, now west, forever following the course of Apollo's chariot as it passed across the sky.

NARCISSUS

Sometimes the gods made transformations just to amuse themselves—neither for punishment nor for the protection of mortals, but just for a little joke.

NARCISSUS FELL IN LOVE WITH A FACE HE SAW IN THE WATER

Narcissus was a youth who was so lovely that he was almost like a girl in his appearance. Like Clytie, he fell in love and pined without eating, day after day.

It was not a beautiful nymph whom Narcissus loved, nor a dryad, nor an oread, nor even a Greek maiden.

He fell in love with a face he saw in the water. He thought it the face of a beautiful water sprite. Never leaving the bank, he pleaded with the lovely being, begging her to come out of the water and speak to him. Of course, it was only his own face that he saw reflected in the water.

The nymph Echo loved Narcissus. She hid herself near him, and answered as he talked to the face in the water.

When he said, "You are beautiful," Echo replied ever so softly, "You are beautiful," and poor Narcissus thought it was the water sprite who spoke. When he said, "I love you," the voice answered and, as he reached his arm into the water, instantly the face would vanish.

Then Narcissus thought the water nymph had fled from him. So he would call again and again, watching the water until it grew smooth and the face returned. All the time Echo would answer him in her sweet voice.

Echo would have told Narcissus he was in love with his own reflection, but she was being punished by Juno for talking too much. She could not speak unless someone else spoke first, and then only the same words she had heard.

Narcissus stayed by the river, all the time growing thinner and more unhappy. The gods came by in different forms and watched him. They listened to the strange conversation between Narcissus and Echo and thought it funny.

They laughed about it together when they gathered on Mt. Olympus. Just as a bit of fun, when Narcissus grew so thin that he was ready to die, the gods changed him into a beautiful flower, which leaned forever over the river bank to look at its reflection in the water.

PHAETON AND THE CHARIOT OF THE SUN

nce, on their way from school, two Greek boys began to quarrel.

"IS APOLLO INDEED MY FATHER?"

"You are nobody!" said one. "Who is your father?"

"My father is Phoebus Apollo, god of the sun. He drives the four great horses of the day. He lights the earth and the heavens with his light, and I, Phaeton, am his son."

His comrade laughed loudly at his boast. He could not believe that the father of Phaeton, his schoolmate, was Apollo, the god of the sun. He

"O LIGHT OF THE BOUNDLESS WORLD, PHOEBUS, MY FATHER!"

called the other boys together and told them Phaeton's story. They crossed their fingers at him and made all manner of fun of the boy for pretending to be the son of a god.

Phaeton, his cheeks flaming with anger, ran home and burst into his mother's chamber. He told her what had happened.

"Is Apollo indeed my father?" he demanded. "How can I be sure, how can I find proof?"

Clymene, his mother, smiled and drew him to her side. She told him again of the glories of Apollo, as she had often told him before.

"Soon," she said, "you will wish to go yourself to the land where the sun rises and find him where he sits on his throne of light, with the four seasons beside him and the hours and the days grouped nearby. Why not journey there and see for yourself, and find proof that Apollo is your father?"

So, although Clymene grieved to have him leave her, she made him ready for the journey and bade him a loving farewell.

He traveled many days through gray and barren lands, over mountains and across streams, until at length he reached the land of the rising sun and saw afar off the flaming light which glowed about the palace of his father.

As he drew nearer he saw that the columns of the palace were of gold and ivory, upholding a jeweled roof. The steps leading to the entrance shone with every kind of precious stone.

Phaeton entered the palace, and there on his golden throne in the great central hall, surrounded by a wonderful white light, he saw Apollo, clad in pale purple, beautiful and dazzling.

On the sun god's right stood Spring, her head crowned with flowers, and Summer, with poppies in her hair. On his left stood Autumn, wreathed in grapes, and aged Winter, bowed over with the weight of ice and snow.

Apollo looked down and saw the boy as he drew near, his hand shielding his eyes. He knew in a moment that this was his son Phaeton, and laid aside the rays that shone about his head, so that Phaeton might not be blinded by their brightness.

"O light of the boundless world, Phoebus, my father!" Phaeton cried. "If you are indeed my parent, give me some proof by which I may be known as your son."

Apollo stretched out his hand to Phaeton and drew him nearer. He looked at him, so straight and brave and young, and the sun god was proud of him.

"My son," he said, "for proof, ask of me what you wish and it shall be given."

Phaeton at once thought of the chariot of the sun. He pictured himself riding across the sky holding the reins of his father's horses. He imagined the amazement of his friends if they could see him.

"Let me for one day drive the chariot of the sun," he answered. "Let me ride from morning until evening thro ugh the clouds in your chariot, holding the reins of your four horses."

THE HORSES LEFT THE TRAVELED ROAD AND DASHED HEADLONG IN AMONG THE STARS

Apollo was sorry that he had made Phaeton so rash a promise, and begged him to choose something else. He reminded the boy that he was not yet grown, and that he was only mortal. He told of the dreadful dangers that every day surrounded the chariot on both its upward and its downward path.

"The first part of the way," he said, "is so steep that the horses can barely climb it, and the last part descends so rapidly that I can hardly hold them. Besides, the heaven itself is always turning, hurrying with it the stars, and always I am afraid lest it sweep me from the chariot and carry the horses from the road. The way leads through the abode of frightful monsters. You must pass the horns of the Bull, the Lion's jaws, the Scorpion, and the Crab.

"O Phaeton," he begged, "look around the world and choose whatever you wish that is precious, whether in the sea or in the midst of the earth, and it shall be yours; but give up this longing to drive my chariot, which can mean only death to you, and destruction."

"No," said Phaeton, "I do not care for anything either in the sea or on the earth. I want only to drive the chariot of Phoebus, my father."

So Phoebus Apollo sadly led the way to the chariot. It was of gold, with a seat of jewels, and around it flamed such a blaze of light that for a moment Phaeton feared to go nearer, it seemed so fiery and scorching.

Rosy-fingered Dawn threw open the silver doors of the East, and there before him Phaeton saw the stars fading away, and the moon, her nightly journey finished, hurrying from the sky. The four great chargers were led from their stalls, and Phaeton cried out in delight as he saw their arched necks and stamping feet. Fire poured from their nostrils, and their hoofs were shod with light.

Phoebus bathed the boy's face with a powerful oil so that he would not be burned, set the rays of the sun on his head, and bade him hold tight to the reins, keep to the middle of the road, and follow the tracks of the wheels.

"Go not too high," he warned, "or you will burn the heavenly dwellings; nor too low, or you will set the earth on fire."

Phaeton joyfully grasped the reins and, holding his head high with delight and pride, rode into the purple path of the morning sky.

THE SCORPION REACHED HIS GREAT CLAWS TOWARDS THE CHARIOT

The horses darted forward with mighty strength and scattered the clouds. Soon they felt that the touch on the reins was not their master's, but a lighter one, and that the chariot itself was not so heavy. So, filling the air with their fiery snorting, they sped on faster and faster, while Phaeton tried to hold them back.

They left the traveled road and dashed headlong in among the stars. Phaeton was borne along like the petal of a flower by the wind, and knew not how to guide his fiery steeds. Looking down, he saw the earth spreading below, and his knees grew weak with fright. He wished that he had never left his mother or asked to drive the chariot of the sun.

Around him on every side were the monsters of the sky. The Scorpion reached his great claws toward the chariot as it passed, and

HIS HAIR ON FIRE, PHAETON FELL HEADLONG LIKE A STREAK OF LIGHTNING

Phaeton dropped the reins. The horses galloped off into unknown regions of the sky, now high up toward the abode of the gods, now downward, so close to the earth that the mountains caught fire, the Alps covered with snow grew hot, and the Apennines flamed.

The earth cracked open. Grassy plains were scorched into deserts. Even the sea shrank, and the fishes and water nymphs hurried down to the deepest parts of the ocean.

So terrible was the heat that Mother Earth cried out to Jupiter, "O ruler of the gods, I can no more supply fruits for men, or herbage for cattle, and my brother Ocean suffers with me. Your own heaven is smoking, and your clouds are on fire. If sea, earth, and heaven burn, we fall again into Chaos. Oh, take thought for our deliverance!"

Then Jupiter mounted the tower on Olympus, from which he shook his thunderbolts and his forked lightning. He hurled a mighty bolt at the chariot and poured rain on the smoking earth until the fires were extinguished.

Poor Phaeton, still clinging to the reeling chariot as it swayed across the sky, was struck by Jupiter's thunderbolt and, his hair on fire, fell headlong like a streak of lightning into the river Eridanus, which soothed him and cooled his burning body.

Jason and the Golden Fleece

There was once a young prince named Jason. His parents ruled over Iolcus, in Thessaly. Their kingdom was filled with happiness and peace, for they were wise and good and noble.

CHIRON THE CENTAUR

But one day the King's brother, Pelias, came riding at the head of an army. He made war on Iolcus, and took the kingdom from Jason's father. Pelias had evil in his heart, and would have killed his brother and Prince Jason, but they fled and hid themselves among lowly people who loved them.

Now, there was at this time a strange and wonderful school in the mountains of Thessaly, a school where the princes of Greece were taught and made strong of body and brave of heart.

Chiron, the centaur, kept this school and reared the young princes. He taught them how to hunt and to fight and to sing, how to take care of their bodies and to bear themselves according to their birth.

So Jason, being still a little boy, was sent to this wonderful school. Here he grew up with the other Greek princes of his age.

At last came the time when Chiron told him the story of the evil King Pelias, who had stolen the kingdom of Iolcus and had driven Jason's father from his throne.

Jason was brown and strong and hardened by Chiron's training. He girded on his sword and set out to take the kingdom away from Pelias.

It was early in spring, and as he journeyed he came to a swollen stream and saw an aged woman gazing in despair at the waters she could not cross.

Jason remembered his training as a prince, and offered to carry her across. He lifted her to his back and she gave him her staff for support. He stepped into the swift-running stream, which no one else had dared cross and although he bent under the weight of his burden he fought bravely against the waters with all his strength.

At last he reached the opposite bank and set the old woman on the grass. Suddenly, in a flash of light, she was transformed into the glorious figure of Juno, queen of the gods. At her feet stood a peacock. Its purple and blue and green tail feathers swept over the grass and its shining head rested against her hand.

The goddess promised aid and protection to Jason forever after, and vanished as quickly as she had appeared. So in all his undertakings Jason was watched over and blessed by Juno in return for his kindness to her.

At last Jason reached Iolcus and demanded the throne from Pelias. That crafty and wicked old King did not refuse him at once. A banquet was prepared, and with every appearance of kindness, King Pelias did honor to young Jason. The King feasted him and seemed to welcome him to Iolcus, but in reality he planned his death.

While they ate, the bards gathered around the hall and sang of heroes and brave deeds, as bards were accustomed to sing at banquets of kings.

They sang of the story of Phrixus and Helle, the two Greek children who escaped from their wicked stepmother, riding on the back of Mercury's golden-fleeced ram. They sang of how Nephele, the real mother, weeping and heavy of heart, placed her little son and daughter on the ram's back and watched them as they sped away from Thessaly. The ram leapt into the air and flew through the clouds as if he had wings. They passed over the sea toward Colchis, the kingdom of their uncle, where they knew they would be safe.

The bards touched their lute strings sadly, and sang of how little Helle became frightened, as she looked down upon the tossing sea, and how she fell from the ram's back into the water, which ever after was called Hellespont.

But Phrixus clung fast and reached Colchis in safety. He offered the ram as a thanks-offering to the gods, and hung the Golden Fleece high on an oak tree, setting a fearful dragon to guard it.

Here after all the years it still hung, waiting for some young hero to come and conquer and claim it.

The bards sang of the glory of the Fleece, of its glittering richness, and of the heroes who had died seeking it. Pelias noticed how Jason's eyes were shining. He knew that the song had moved him and rightly guessed that Jason longed to go in search of this Golden Fleece.

Pelias thought that this would be a good way to bring about Jason's death. The dragon had killed many other youths who had been rash enough to seek the Golden Fleece, and Pelias felt certain that Jason would perish also. So he leaned toward the young prince and urged him to set out on the adventure and bring back the Fleece which rightfully belonged to Thessaly.

Jason sprang from his seat and vowed that he would go.

First he visited Juno's temple and asked for help on his journey. She gave him the limb of a mighty and wonderful oak for the figurehead of his boat, which would speak to him in time of danger, and advise and warn him on his voyage.

THE RAM LEAPT INTO THE AIR AND FLEW THROUGH THE CLOUDS AS IF HE HAD WINGS

JUNO SPED THEM ON THEIR WAY WITH FAVORABLE WINDS

Then Juno bade Minerva provide a swift-sailing vessel, made from the wood of pine trees which grew on Mount Pelion.

Jason called his vessel the Argo, and sent for the young princes of Chiron's school to come with him and help in the search for the Golden Fleece.

Hercules came and also Admetus, Theseus, Orpheus, Castor, and Pollux, all the bravest and noblest heroes of Greece, anxious to take part in this adventure and to bring the Golden Fleece back to Thessaly.

Juno sped them on their way with favorable winds, and the Argo sailed swiftly toward Colchis. When danger threatened, the branch of

MEDEA WAS SKILLED IN ALL MANNER OF ENCHANTMENTS AND MAGIC

the talking oak spoke wise words of help and counsel. It guided them safely between the clashing rocks of the Symplegades, and past the land of the cruel Harpies. So they came at last, after many adventures, to Colchis, the kingdom of Eetes. Now the Fleece had hung for so long in his realm that King Eetes was unwilling to part with it. Like Pelias, he was crafty and full of wiles, and did not refuse Jason, but agreed to give him the Fleece on certain conditions.

First Jason must catch and harness two wild, fire-breathing bulls, then plough a stony field, sacred to Mars. After that he must sow the field with dragon's teeth and conquer the host of armed men which would grow from them. Last of all, he must overcome the dragon which coiled around the foot of the oak and guarded the Fleece.

Jason feared that these tasks were impossible for any mortal to fulfil without the help of the gods. So he hurried down to the vessel to speak with the branch of the talking oak. On his way he met Medea, the princess of Colchis. She was young and beautiful and skilled in all manner of enchantments and magic. Her heart was filled with kindness toward the brave young stranger and she wished to help him.

She gave Jason her strongest charms and her wisest counsel. By the aid of Medea's magic he caught the fiery bulls as they came roaring from their pasture. He harnessed them and drove them over the stony field, and made them drag the heavy plough which turned the earth in dark furrows.

Eetes was amazed, for no one had ever yoked or harnessed these bulls before.

When the field was ready, Jason asked for the dragon's teeth, and Eetes gave them to him in a helmet. Up and down the long furrows he sowed them, and when the last one was in the ground, he ploughed the earth again, and covered them and waited.

Long rows of shining spears began to pierce the ground and to

JASON AND THE FIERY BULLS

shoot up into the air. Then rose the plumed helmets of a thousand soldiers; then their shields, and their bodies.

They stood, full armed and fierce, looking over the field. When they beheld Jason, they ran toward him with waving spears and a clatter of shields.

From his pocket Jason took a magic stone which Medea had given him. He threw it into the midst of the thousand soldiers; it fell among them like discord itself. Each soldier thought another had thrown it, and each man began to fight his neighbor. More and more furiously they fought. Soon the ploughed field was covered with fallen soldiers. They continued to kill one another until not one was left.

ALL THE SOLDIERS STOOD FULL ARMED AND FIERCE

Then Medea led Jason to the sacred grove where the dragon watched beside the Fleece. The huge monster rose up, roaring terribly, as Jason approached. He breathed clouds of smoke and fire and lashed his tail against the oak tree.

Jason bravely advanced until he was so near that he could feel the heat of the flames that poured from the dragon's throat. Then he took a magic liquid, which Medea had given him, and threw it straight into the face of the dragon. In a moment the monster fell back to the earth, and coiling himself lazily on the grass, went to sleep.

THE MONSTER COILED HIMSELF LAZILY BENEATH THE TREE

Jason climbed the tree and brought down the wonderful glittering Fleece, then hurried back to his ship.

Because she loved him, Medea left her father's land and sailed away in the Argo with Jason and his comrades. But, sad to relate, they did not live happily ever after, for Medea knew so much sorcery that she was forever practicing new magic and often she brought trouble on herself and Jason.

On the way back to Thessaly they passed through many dangers, but at last, with Juno's help, came safely home.

Jason and his comrades forced the evil King Pelias to give back the throne. Once more the people of Thessaly lived in happiness and peace under the rule of their own rightful king.

PYGMALION AND GALATEA

BEAUTIFUL GIRLS CAME WALKING BY PYGMALION'S WINDOW

Pygmalion was a sculptor who could think of nothing but his chisels and the marble and ivory with which he loved to work. Beautiful Greek girls came walking by his window and peeped in at the door to watch him, but he never raised his head or paid the least attention to them.

PYGMALION SPENT ALL HIS TIME ADMIRING AND ADORING THE FIGURE HE HAD MADE

One day Pygmalion chose the largest, most perfect piece of ivory in the kingdom. When the laborers had brought it to his home, he took his keenest tools and began to carve the ivory with delicate care.

"There is no maiden living," said Pygmalion, "so beautiful as this statue that I shall make."

For weeks he worked, stopping only to eat, and at night to throw himself on the floor beside the statue to rest.

Day by day the figure grew more lovely. At last it seemed so perfect that nothing could be done to make it more wonderful. Still Pygmalion worked, smoothing and carving the ivory until it was indeed more beautiful than any Greek maiden in the land.

When the statue was finished, Pygmalion clothed it in soft garments and hung jewels around the ivory neck. He spent all his time admiring and adoring the figure he had made. He named it "Galatea," which means "Sleeping Love."

Just at this time there was in Pygmalion's city a festival in honor of Venus, the goddess of beauty and of love. Pygmalion went to her temple. He offered gifts at her altar, and prayed that she would give him for his bride a living maiden exactly like his beautiful ivory statue.

Venus had been standing unseen beside her altar. When she heard Pygmalion's prayer, she left her temple and went to the sculptor's home to see the figure of which he was so fond.

The goddess was delighted with the loveliness of Pygmalion's statue. She thought it looked much like herself. This pleased her so that she touched the cold ivory and bade it live.

She laid her fingers on the waving hair and it became soft and lustrous. The cheeks grew pink, the eyes blue, and the lips like coral.

When Pygmalion returned and entered his home, the statue no longer stood in its usual corner. Instead, a beautiful maiden with golden hair and skin like ivory flushed with the color of sunrise walked toward him.

Pygmalion watched in amazement. When he saw that his statue lived and moved, he threw himself on the floor and clasped her feet. They were warm and rosy.

Galatea looked down at him, smiling and touching his hair with her slender fingers.

Pygmalion did not forget to offer thanks to the goddess. He built an altar to Venus of ivory and gold and carved it with all manner of blossoms and birds.

Every day as long as Pygmalion and Galatea lived, they offered gifts at the altar, and Venus in return blessed them with happiness and love.

ERYSICHTHON AND THE OAK TREE

There was once a mortal named Erysichthon who would not believe all the stories of the gods' transformations. He went stamping through the woods, picking flowers and breaking trees. Just by good fortune he happened not to injure any tree that held a nymph or a dryad. But one day he went to chop wood in a sacred grove, and selected the biggest and most beautiful oak tree of all—the tree around which the dryads and wood sprites loved best to play.

The grove belonged to the goddess Ceres, who made the grain and barley grow, and who watched over all the fruits and vegetables. Everyone was especially careful not to make Ceres angry for fear that she might spoil the harvest.

Erysichthon's companions would not touch the trees in Ceres' grove, because they were afraid. But Erysichthon boasted that it did not matter to him if Ceres herself were in a tree, he would cut whichever one he liked.

So he set his axe to the wood. The great oak trembled, and blood flowed from the wound he had made, but Erysichthon paid no heed and kept on chopping.

One of his friends seized Erysichthon's arm and begged him to stop. But Erysichthon struck him with the axe and chopped harder than ever.

THE TREE AROUND WHICH THE DRYADS AND WOOD NYMPHS LOVED BEST TO PLAY

Then a clear sad voice spoke from among the branches. "I am a nymph," said the voice, "and beloved by Ceres. Dying by your hands, I warn you that punishment will be sent you."

The others fled from the grove in terror, but Erysichthon swung his axe until the oak leaned over, creaking and groaning as great trees do when they are felled.

The tree, as it fell, crashed through the grove, and swept a dozen smaller trees to the earth. Erysichthon wiped his forehead and went home to dinner.

The dryads had been watching from behind the trees. Now they went quickly to Ceres and told her what had happened. She was so angry that she called an oread from the mountain and sent her with a message to Famine, who lived far away on a wild crag.

FAMINE FLEW SWIFTLY DOWNWARD FROM HER WILD MOUNTAIN
CRAG TO ERYSICHTHON'S HOUSE

Oreads were mountain nymphs who could travel from one mountain top to another by merely floating across. The oread told Famine what Erysichthon had done, and Famine flew swiftly downward to his house.

Erysichthon had eaten and thrown himself down to rest on his couch when Famine floated into the room unseen and hovered over his head. She folded her black cloak about him and breathed her poison into his veins. While he slept he dreamed of being hungry, and when he wakened shouted loudly for food.

Erysichthon's lovely daughter brought him bread and meat, but when he had eaten it he felt hungrier than ever. He called for more and still felt famished. His daughter brought plate after plate of hot food, wondering more and more at her father's strange appetite.

At last everything in the house was eaten; Erysichthon walked about looking for something more. He went into the garden and ate the vegetables from the ground and the fruit on the trees. He ate the buds of the flowers, and angrily bade his daughter hurry to the fisherman to get some fish, and to the shepherds to have them prepare a lamb. He could think of nothing but eating.

After a few days, Erysichthon had eaten all the food he owned, and spent all of his gold to buy more. He sold his beds and chairs and tables and his daughter's ornaments.

At last he sold his daughter herself to be a servant. When she heard what her father had done she went down to the sea and prayed to Neptune to protect her.

The god of the sea heard her prayer and came quickly to help her. His dolphin bore him over the waves with the speed of the wind, and he changed the daughter of Erysichthon into a young fisherman, so that neither her new master nor her father could find her.

Erysichthon at length died of hunger, and Neptune changed his daughter once more into her own form.

NIOBE

There was once a queen named Niobe. She was rich and very proud of her beautiful kingdom and her many possessions, but especially of her seven sons and seven daughters.

Niobe clothed them in linen of purple and scarlet. Her handmaidens embroidered their robes with rich patterns. They wore jewels and ornaments of gold. When the seven princes and their sisters went walking together, they looked like a moving garden of bright poppies.

One day the people of Thebes held a festival in honor of the goddess Latona, who was the mother of Diana and Apollo. The women and children put on their best robes and wore wreaths of laurel on their heads. They carried offerings of flowers and fragrant oils to the altar in Latona's temple.

Niobe, riding through Thebes in her chariot, watched them on their way to the festival. Usually, as Niobe's chariot passed, the people threw flowers before her and bowed low in honor of their queen. But today they bowed less deeply and hurried on to the temple, carrying their flowers to the goddess.

Niobe drove to the temple and watched them enter.

"What folly is this?" she asked. "Why should Latona be honored with worship and none be paid to me?"

THE WOMEN AND CHILDREN CARRIED OFFERINGS AND FLOWERS

"This is the day of Latona's festival," they answered. "We pay homage to her, for she is the mother of Apollo, god of the sun, and of Diana, who guides the moon."

At this, Niobe compared her own fourteen children with Latona's two. Like all mothers, she thought her children more beautiful and wiser and more glorious than any other children. She drew herself up with pride and anger and spoke to her people.

"I, your queen," she said, "have fourteen children, seven sons and seven daughters. Were I to lose some of my children, I should still be richer than Latona, who has only two. Put off the laurel from your brows—have done with this worship!"

When Niobe spoke no one dared disobey. They put down their burdens of flowers and their gifts. They took off their wreaths of laurel and, leaving Latona's tempel strewn with unplaced offerings, they returned to their homes.

Niobe drove proudly away to her palace, not knowing that Latona herself had been present, invisible in the temple. She had come to attend the festival, and was now filled with a great anger against Niobe for interrupting the worshipers.

APOLLO AND DIANA TOOK THEIR SHARPEST ARROWS AND WENT TO A HILL OVERLOOKING THEBES

She returned to the Cynthian mountaintop where she dwelt. There she sought her children, Diana and Apollo, and told them to punish Niobe for her sin. Apollo and Diana took their sharpest arrows and went to a hill overlooking the city of Thebes.

On the wide plain outside the city Niobe's seven sons were engaged in different sports. Ismenos, the eldest, was driving his chariot. An arrow struck him as he guided his foaming steeds, and dropping the reins he fell lifeless.

One brother now fled, urging his horses to greater speed, but an arrow overtook him as he rode. Another ran to his aid, and fell. Two brothers were wrestling, and one arrow pierced them both.

ONE OF NIOBE'S YOUNGER SONS SAT WATCHING HIS BROTHERS

AGAIN NIOBE AND HER DAUGHTERS HEARD THE SOUND OF A BOW

One of the younger boys sat watching his elder brothers from a little distance. He was astonished at their fall, and thought this was some strange new game. But another arrow sped from Apollo's bow, and he fell backward and lay lifeless like the others.

Only one was left, Ilioneus. He prayed to the gods to save him. Apollo would have spared Ilioneus but the arrow had already left the string, and it was too late.

Then Niobe, sitting in her palace, heard sounds of wailing and mourning. Her attendants came to tell her what had happened. She rushed to the plain with her daughters and found the bodies of her seven sons stretched where they had fallen.

Although she could not see Diana and Apollo, she guessed that this terrible punishment had come from the gods. But her spirit was still proud. She gathered her seven daughters close to her and, raising her eyes to heaven, cried out:

"Cruel Latona! Satisfy your rage with my suffering. Yet, great as is my loss, I am still richer than you, my conqueror."

Again they heard the sound of a bow, and Diana's arrow flew through the air. And now one after another Niobe's lovely daughters dropped beside her until only the youngest was left.

Niobe was proud no longer. She fell on her knees, and with one arm around the little princess, stretched the other toward the hill from which the arrows had come.

"Spare me this last and youngest child," she cried. But the arrow had left Diana's bow, and in a moment the youngest princess lay beside the others. Niobe never left the plain, but bowed her head and wept day after day until at last the gods pitied her grief and changed her into a rock. But still she wept, and ever afterward a tiny stream trickled from the stone, the sign of her never-ending sorrow.

TO EACH BIRD AND ANIMAL EPIMETHEUS GAVE A GIFT

PROMETHEUS AND THE FIRE OF THE GODS

Prometheus and Epimetheus were Titans, who lived on the earth before men were created. The Titans were large and strong and could do many wonderful things.

Prometheus knew that the first men were soon coming to live on earth, and spent most of his time, like a great father, making things ready for their coming.

He planted the first seeds of fruit trees and of flowers. He opened up tiny springs on the sides of the mountains so that little streams might come running down and water the valleys. He watched over the animals and taught his brother, Epimetheus, how to help him.

To each bird and animal Epimetheus gave a gift that would make it more useful or more beautiful. He gave wool to the sheep, and soft fur to many small animals so that man might have clothing. He gave milk to the cow, and speed to the horse, ivory tusks to the elephant, whalebone to the whale, beautiful feathers to the ostrich, and sweet songs to the birds—all things that mankind has ever since found pleasant and useful.

Last of all he decided to have ready some especially splendid gift for man himself. Prometheus tried to think of something great and beautiful enough and at last he remembered the fire of the gods.

"If," thought he, "I could go up to the sun and light a torch, perhaps I could bring fire to earth for man to use."

So he climbed to the top of Mount Olympus, the home of the gods. Its tall peaks reached up into the sky, so steep that only a god or a Titan might ascend.

From the very highest point Prometheus stepped off among the clouds. Then, walking carefully from one fleecy island to another, he approached the chariot of the sun as it sped across the sky, driven by Apollo and drawn by the four horses of the Day.

No man could have endured the heat from the chariot as it drew near, but Prometheus was a Titan. Stretching toward the chariot a long torch, he held it tightly as it caught fire although the light blinded him and the fire burned his hands. Apollo passed on his way, never guessing that Prometheus had stolen some of the heavenly fire.

Hiding his torch as much as he could, Prometheus hurried down the mountain of the gods until he reached the earth. There he kindled a fire among the rocks and bade Epimetheus watch it, so that it might never die out.

When man was born on earth, he used the fire to warm himself, to cook his food, and to frighten away the fiercest of the animals when they prowled too near at night. He learned to use fire to bake his clay dishes so that they would hold water, and to melt gold from the rocks.

But Jupiter was angry with Prometheus for daring to steal fire from the sun, and just when man had learned to enjoy the gift of Prometheus, the god snatched it away. He forbade Prometheus ever again to approach the sun. For a long time Prometheus considered how he might regain fire for man, who was now miserable indeed, for he had no way of cooking his food or of warming himsel

Prometheus again set out for Mount Olympus, but this time he visited Vulcan's workshop, and took some fire from his forge. He hid the stolen flame in a hollow reed so that the gods might not see it, and hurried back to earth.

JUPITER CHAINED PROMETHEUS TO A ROCK ON MOUNT CAUCASUS

Jupiter, looking down from Olympus, saw smoke again ascending from the earth. He was so angry that he dropped his thunderbolts, raged down from the mountain, and ordered Prometheus to put out the fires.

Prometheus refused. So Jupiter chained him to a rock on Mount Caucasus and tormented him in many ways.

PANDORA'S BOX

After Prometheus had been taken away and chained, Epimetheus was very lonely. Men loved him as boys love their father, and came to him for help in everything. But Epimetheus wanted someone to live with him and cheer him, because he often became sad, remembering how his brother Prometheus had been bound to the rock. Even Jupiter himself began to be sorry for Epimetheus, and decided to call the gods together in council.

There was one god who wore beautiful silver sandals with white wings growing from the heels. These sandals gave him such speed that he had only to rise into the air and take one great flying leap, and in a moment's time he would be at the other side of the sky. This god's name was Mercury; sometimes he was called the "Speedy-Comer." He was the messenger of all the others, and Jupiter now sent him to summon the gods.

Apollo left his chariot and came quickly at Jupiter's command. Vulcan, the craftsman of Olympus, laid down his anvil and his goldsmith's tools. But he came more slowly, for he was lame and could not hurry.

Venus, goddess of love and beauty, with her little son Cupid, came floating through the clouds. Juno, with her peacock, took her place at Jupiter's side. Minerva, the goddess of wisdom, came also. All the deities of Olympus ranged themselves at the right and left of Jupiter's throne to consider what might be done for Epimetheus.

THIS GOD'S NAME WAS MERCURY

They decided that Epimetheus must have a companion. Mercury was sent to the earth to bring back some soft clay. In a moment he returned with it. Vulcan, the artist of the gods, then took the clay in his hands and began to form a beautiful figure, while Jupiter looked on and told him just how he thought the companion should be made. Soon

VENUS, GODDESS OF LOVE AND BEAUTY, WITH HER LITTLE SON CUPID,
CAME FLOATING THROUGH THE CLOUDS

Vulcan had finished modeling a lovely clay form, not quite like that of man, but more delicate.

Now Venus touched the clay figure and it became ivory white. The waves of soft hair which Vulcan had modeled became fine gold. Jupiter breathed on the lips and life entered the form. Her blue eyes opened, and the gods, seeing her so lovely, came nearer and gave her beautiful gifts.

Apollo, who could play sweetly on the lyre, gave her the gift of music. Mercury gave her a gentle voice and the art of knowing how to speak. They named her Pandora, which means "All-Gifted."

Venus gave her a blue robe with rich embroidery, and Mercury led her down from Mount Olympus to be a comrade for Epimetheus on the earth. Pandora was delighted with the flowers, the birds, and the sweet fruits that grew around her. She played and laughed so much that Epimetheus grew happier, and forgot that he had ever been sad.

Now, everything would have been perfect had it not been for Pandora's curiosity. There was a chest in Epimetheus' house which he kept tied with a strong cord. When she asked if she might open the chest, he told her that Mercury had left it, that it did not belong to them, and must not be touched. But Pandora was so curious that she continued to beg and tease Epimetheus to open the chest and look inside.

"If Mercury brought it before I came," she said, "perhaps it is full

WITH A BUZZ AND A ROAR THERE FLEW OUT OF THE BOX A SWARM OF LITTLE EVIL-LOOKING CREATURES

of dresses and shining sandals and things for me. O Epimetheus, let me have just one look!"

But Epimetheus continued to shake his head and say "No," and Pandora pouted and grew more unhappy and curious all the time.

At last one day when Epimetheus was out, Pandora carefully untied the cord that fastened the lid, then opened the chest. With a buzz and a roar, there flew out a swarm of little, evil-looking, stinging creatures, wildly turning somersaults and leaping with gladness at being free.

They were not pleasant to look at, and Pandora was frightened as she saw them go flying out of the house. In a few moments Epimetheus came running and shouting, with all the men and boys after him, crying out and quarreling and making a dreadful noise.

"Pandora, Pandora!" cried Epimetheus. "You have let loose all the evils and troubles that were in the chest!"

Pandora wept to see Epimetheus so angry. She was sorry that she had ever touched the chest. Epimetheus did not stay to comfort her, but hurried out again and tried to stop the wailing and quarreling.

As Pandora wept and listened to the strange, dreadful sounds outside, a soft hand touched her on the shoulder. She turned quickly and saw a little silvery-white figure, no bigger than the troubles had been, but beautiful and kind looking.

"I am still with you," said the little creature. "You can never be altogether unhappy if I stay; for my name is Hope."

Very gently she flew to Pandora's wrist, and Pandora ran to the door and held her hand high, so that everyone might see. One by one the boys and men looked up and saw the little figure of Hope.

Soon the quarreling and wailing stopped, and then Epimetheus sent them back to their homes. Ever after, although all the little troubles still flew around the earth to bother them, hope was always somewhere near to help and give them comfort.